The Ballet Shoes in Syria

CATHERINE BRUTON

First published in the UK in 2019 by Nosy Crow Ltd

The Crow's Nest, 14 Baden Place
Crosby Row, London, SE1 1YW, UK

www.nosycrow.com

ISBN: 978 1 78800 4 503

Nosy Crow and associated logos are trademarks and/or registered trademarks of Nosy Crow Ltd

A CIP catalogue record for this book is available from the British Library.

Printed and bound in Great Britain by Clays Ltd, Elcograf S.p.A.
Typeset by Tiger Media

Papers used by Nosy Crow are made from wood grown in sustainable forests

5 7 9 10 8 6 4

For Evie

And for the 11.5 million refugee children around the globe who have been forced from their homes and are currently seeking safe haven.

C.B.

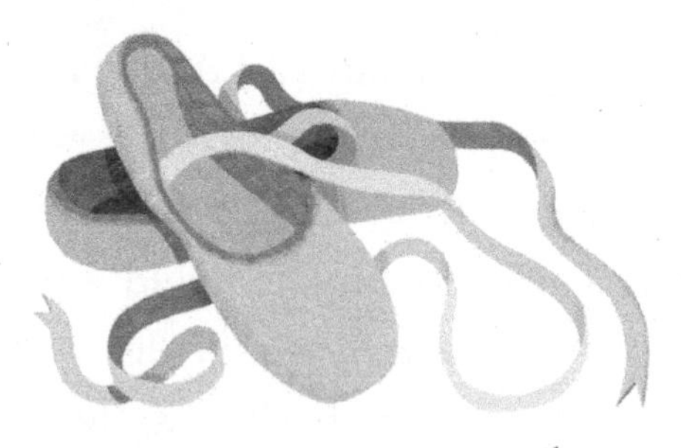

Chapter 1

Aya could hear the music floating through the walls. And the woman's voice: "One, two … *port de bras* … lift those arms, girls … three, four … straighter – yes! … five, six … eeeee-longate…" The notes of the piano seemed to trickle down through Aya's limbs, and her fingertips moved involuntarily towards the tune that tinkled through the stuffy air.

The music stopped. Aya wiggled her toes and glanced around. The community centre was crowded – a jumble-sale collection of people, talking in a bustle of different languages. Hot sun spilled through dusty windows and the room smelled of soup and unwashed clothing. *And sadness,* Aya thought. She sighed and shifted in her seat.

The music started again and Aya glanced upwards. The piano notes were coming from somewhere close by. Upstairs? If she closed her eyes really tight and focused hard enough she could almost – almost – imagine herself back home, in the dance studio in Aleppo. With the heat on her limbs, the white-hot sun falling through the skylight, and the aromas of the city trickling through the windows – dusty streets, car fumes, incense. She smiled as she remembered standing at the barre, tracing her pointed toe through a series of *rond de jambes*, recalling the dust that sometimes trickled across the floor and that drove Madam Belova mad.

Anyone looking at Aya at that moment would have seen a small girl who looked much younger than her eleven years, holding a sleeping toddler in her arms. She had her eyes closed, and a curious expression danced over her face as her small foot traced circles on the grubby floorboards. A headscarf covered her black hair, and the clothes she was wearing were too big for her – leggings sagged over her skinny limbs and an old dress, which might perhaps have once been her mother's, hung limply off her tiny frame. And yet there was something about the way she sat – the bird-like tilt of her pinched face – that made her seem as if she belonged somewhere different.

The sounds of music stopped once more and Aya wriggled on the hard plastic seat. She was hungry and Moosa was heavy in her arms. The music made her feel fidgety and restless, and something else she couldn't find a word for. She shook her head determinedly and sat up straight – she needed to be focused today. To help Mumma.

"How long do you think it will it be?" she asked the woman next to her, who just shrugged. Aya wasn't sure if she'd even understood.

She glanced around again. They'd been waiting for three hours to talk to the caseworker – a young man with a beard and tired-looking eyes who sat behind a makeshift desk, papers and files piled up around him. Right now he was talking to Mr and Mrs Massoud – the old couple from the hostel who had told Aya that they came from Damascus. Aya heard the words: "Application for asylum … appeal … lawyers … undocumented … hearing."

"Same old story," she muttered to Moosa. "Right, Moos! Over and over – wherever we go."

Moosa shifted in his sleep, making the funny little sucking noises that made Aya want to squeeze him tight. "You sound like a baby rabbit, Moos!" she muttered, planting a kiss on her brother's grubby, tear-stained face. His hair was damp with sweat, his fingers clasped tightly round Aya's thumb. She remembered the first time she had held him, the wave of love she had felt then. The feeling she'd had that she would never let anything happen to him – ever.

"Don't worry, Moosie!" she whispered into his damp cheeks. "Aya's here. Aya is going to sort it all out. Promise."

Mumma was sitting next to her. She looked tired and faraway. "It won't be long now, Mumma," Aya said.

But Mumma did not reply. She just kept staring up at the dusty windows – as if she could see something through them that Aya could not.

"You OK, Mumma?" Aya asked. "You hungry? I can get you some food? There is soup today."

But Mumma said nothing.

Just then the door to the community centre swung open and the music spilled into the room, louder now. A quicker piece was playing and Aya found her toes tapping out the beat on the floor.

"One, two, three… Squeeze, two, three… To the barre, two, three… and – photograph! Loooovely, ladies!"

Aya held her breath for a second. "Photograph!" she muttered, half to herself and half to Moosa.

Madam Belova liked to say that too. "Photograph!" It meant a moment of stillness, a pause, catching hold of the music and waiting with it. The notes and the dancer suspended in time – hovering in the air – just for a second.

Suddenly Aya couldn't sit still a moment longer. She glanced at the queue of people in front of them. It would be ages before they were called. She could slip out – just for a moment – to go and look.

"Mumma, I'm just going out. I won't be long. I promise I'll be back to help. And I'll get you some soup – and bread. You need to eat, OK?"

Mumma turned and nodded, but she seemed to have only half heard. *I will make sure she eats properly today*, Aya said to herself. *And rub her temples the way Dad used to do when she got one of her headaches. And I'll talk to the caseworker and get everything sorted out. Then Mumma will be able to relax – get better. Be herself again.*

Aya carefully uncurled her little brothers' fingers from her own and laid him down gently in the battered pushchair that Sally – the nice young volunteer who ran the centre – had found for them. Then she stood up and did a little spin on the spot, which – just for a moment – made old Mr Abdul sitting opposite think of a curling autumn leaf, falling through the air.

But Aya was unaware of being leaf-like as she made her way over to the doorway.

She just needed to shake off the fidgety feeling that the music had sent trickling through her limbs. Before she burst!

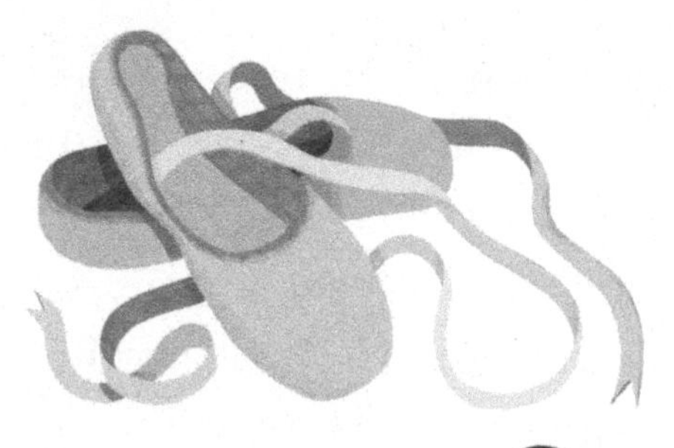

Chapter 2

It was a relief to be out of there. Away from the smell of old clothes, boiled vegetables, and that other smell, which Aya had decided was sadness. Once upon a time she'd have said that sadness didn't have a smell. Now it was more familiar than the fast-fading scents of home. Worse than the smell of Moosa's stinky nappies, worse than Dad's smelly socks, worse than the boys' changing room at school – though she wouldn't have thought that was possible a year ago!

Aya stretched her arms high above her head and looked around the lobby. Manchester Welcomes Refugees was housed in a community centre in a run-down area of the city, where crumbling red-brick terraces crouched in the shadows of dying and derelict tower blocks. So different from the tree-lined streets and sunlit avenues of Aleppo – before the war, that is.

There were posters on the notice board advertising all the other things that went on here. Aya ran her eyes over the confusing words: "Latin and Ballroom Club – All Ages Welcome" … "Hor-ti-cul-tur-al Society" (she sounded out the syllables) … "Zumba Gold" (what was Zumba, anyway?) … "Pilates for Mindfulness" (she had no idea what that meant either!).

Aya remembered sitting at the kitchen table with Dad teaching her English, laughing at the strange-sounding syllables. She could still see Dad's smiling face – the dark almond eyes, the hint of grey in the stubble on his chin, the small scar on his cheek from when he'd had chicken pox as a child. She pushed the thought away quickly. She couldn't think about Dad. Not if she was going to keep it together.

The music was much clearer out here and Aya could hear the woman's voice – speaking English with a slight foreign lilt to it. "Ladies, are we swans on the lake or the ugly ducklings? Let me see grace. Let me see elegance. LOV-ER-LY!"

The music, the voice, the soft thud of feet moving in time seemed to tug at something inside Aya. Like the strings on a tightly bound package, loosening memories she normally buried deep, deep inside.

"Arms, ladies, arms … and fiiiingers! Feel it in every sinew – right to the tips of your pinkie fingers!"

Aya couldn't help it – she just wanted to look.

She made her way to the staircase and up to the little upstairs lobby. There were benches all around, scattered with a collection of bags and coats and items of clothing. One door seemed to lead to a small office, another led out on to a fire escape. Then there was a pair of white doors with little windows on the top, through which the music was coming. Aya hesitated. It had been so long since she had danced … a whole lifetime ago … another life, almost.

Standing on tiptoe, she could make out a rather battered-looking dance studio, mirrors along one wall and a barre stretching the whole way round. A group of girls were lined up, dressed in black leotards with pink socks and satin shoes. Each girl had her hair pulled back in a bun, though some were neater than others, Aya noticed, as she watched their legs and arms moving in time to the music.

"Straight up like a chocolate finger, la-dies… And no wiggle-waggling as you close!" the teacher was saying. "Now you can all take your hands off the barre – except Miss Dotty, who is seeming to be drunk today, I think."

Aya watched as the girl at the front of the line – who had skin like melted chocolate, a lopsided bun and a mischievous twinkle in her eye – wobbled even more precariously. The girl (who must be Dotty?) put her hand on the barre to steady herself, biting her lip as if to stop giggling.

"Now, squee-eeze in those bottoms and make your necks very long – like the giraffes…" the teacher was saying, walking down the row of girls.

"Very nice, Ciara!" she said to a slender blonde dancer with limbs like snowy branches.

"No see-sawing, Lilli-Ella," to a small girl with mousey hair.

"Don't be making the examiner feel seasick, Grace." This was to a tall girl with sloping shoulders and glasses perched on her nose.

There was no sand on the floor, and the sky through the windows was English blue, not Syrian gold, but otherwise Aya could have been back in Aleppo. Back at home – before the war – before … everything. And it could have been her own classmates lined up at the barre: Samia, Kimi, and Nadiya and Nooda – the twins who always did everything – everything – together, even going to the toilet.

What had happened to the twins?

The teacher turned and Aya could see her properly now. She was old – very old – and tiny, with a snowy-white head of hair pulled into a bun, and a face round and bright like a wrinkled apple. In a flowing black dress with shiny red character shoes on her tiny feet, she looked each girl up and down with her bright violet-blue eyes, lifting an arm here, touching a head there, just as Madam Belova always used to do.

"Make sure you are speaking with your hands, your toes, your eyes, my dancers!" she was saying. "But, Dotty, do tell your eyes to mind their Ps and Qs!"

Just then the girl called Dotty glanced towards the door and caught sight of Aya. A quizzical expression flitted over her face as she held Aya's glance. She smiled and just for a second it looked as if she was going to laugh.

The final notes of the music tinkled out and the barre exercise came to an end. The girls relaxed into easy chatter, reaching for water bottles, sorting out hair and pulling up socks as they made their way to the middle of the floor.

Only the girl called Dotty kept her gaze trained on Aya. And as she took a glug of water she winked and grinned.

Aya smiled back. For the first time in months she

didn't feel invisible.

Aleppo, Syria

Aya barely remembered how the war had begun. She must have been small – six or seven maybe. She had a memory of Dad watching the demonstrations on the TV one evening. He had some of his friends from the hospital over and they were talking, arguing about recent events – the protests on the streets of the capital, the arrests, the fighting... They didn't seem to agree about what was going on. She heard words like "political reforms ... civil rights ... the release of prisoners ... arrests." Words she didn't really understand, but that had ugly shapes to them.

"They are angry at the president," Mumma had explained. Aya wasn't sure if she was talking about the crowds of protestors, or about Dad's friends.

Over the next few days she stared at the images on the news. Fighting in the streets of the capital, Damascus. Protestors waving banners, clashing with police. Shots fired, blood on the streets.

"Why are they so angry, Dadda?" she asked.

"They want to make Syria a better country, habibti,*" said Dad, rubbing the grey stubble on his chin thoughtfully.*

"So why are the police hurting them?"

Dad sighed. "Perhaps people have different versions of better."

She had looked hard at him then. His almond-shaped eyes

looked troubled and he was not smiling. Dad always smiled. Even when he came home exhausted from a long shift at the hospital. He always had a smile for his Aya. For his little dancing girl.

"Will the fighting come here?" she asked. "To Aleppo?"

"I hope not, habibti,*" he said. "I hope not. But if it does, I will keep you and Mumma safe. I promise."*

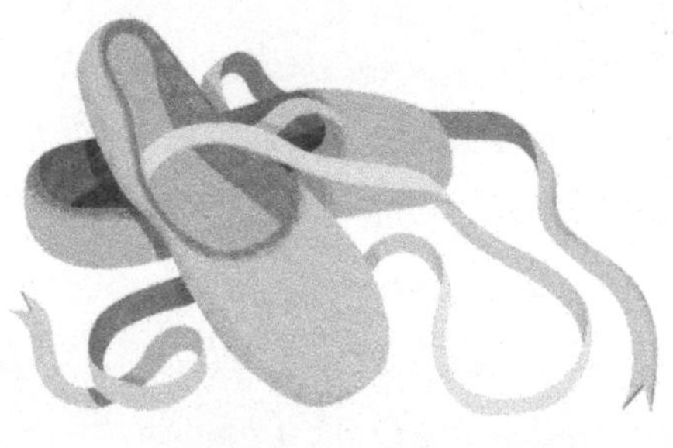

Chapter 3

That night, back in the hostel, Aya could not sleep. The bed she shared with Mumma and Moosa was lumpy, the springs collapsed in one section. The walls were so paper-thin that they could hear everything that was going on in every other room. The family next door were arguing loudly in a language Aya did not understand – the husband shouting, the wife crying. In the room above, a baby wailed, and from somewhere down the corridor she could hear the sound of old Mrs Massoud crying. Poor Mrs Massoud was always crying – for her son who had been taken by government troops in Damascus, and for her daughter, who had been killed by the bombs shortly after. She told Aya that a mother's fountain of tears flows forever.

But tonight there was also music coming from somewhere down the hall – a man's voice singing a song in a language that Aya didn't understand. It made her think of the girls in the dance class. The girl called Dotty who had grinned at her like she was just a normal kid. And Ciara, with the blonde hair and the haughty expression, and the mousey-haired girl – Lilli-Ella – who stuck her tongue out when she was concentrating. Aya's limbs itched as she remembered. Just thinking about it made her want to dance.

"Not really enough room for that kind of thing in here, eh, Moos!" she whispered to her little brother, who lay like a starfish next to her, his tiny fist clamped tightly round her finger, breathing snottily in his sleep.

She glanced at Mumma, asleep on a chair in the corner, her face creased into its usual anxious frown. Then she pulled a blanket over Moosa and climbed out of bed, reaching as quietly as she could for her rucksack.

They hadn't been able to bring much when they left Syria. They had fled in a hurry with only the clothes they were wearing and one bag each. Sometimes Aya thought of her room at home and all the treasures she liked to collect: the posters of ballerinas on her wall, the glass animals on her mantelpiece, the pile of cuddly toys on the rocking chair, the tiny snow globe with a dancer frozen in arabesque that Dad had found in the old market … all the things she'd left behind. In comparison, this room – with its single lightbulb, bare walls, ripped curtains and the damp patch on the ceiling – felt more like a prison cell than a home.

"It doesn't have to be for long," she had said to Mumma when the lady from the centre first showed them in. "And after the appeal we'll find somewhere better. Make a proper home – I promise!"

Another promise.

Aya reached to the bottom of the rucksack, where she had packed the ballet shoes. They were wrapped in a couple of plastic bags to keep them dry, and as she unfolded them she could feel the soft satin under her fingers. She hadn't looked at them or touched them for months, but holding them now made her smile. Dad had bought them for her, just a few weeks before they left. Her first pair of pointe shoes – the most beautiful things she had ever owned. She had no idea where he'd managed to get them from. But Dad was like that. He could do stuff other dads couldn't.

She remembered dancing in them for the very first time, in the kitchen at home. Patterned linoleum underfoot; Dad sitting at the table with Moosa in his arms; Mumma standing by the sink, hands wet, clapping with delight and laughing about her beautiful ballerina. "Dance for us, Aya!" Dad had said.

Mumma sat up, alert suddenly – the frightened look in her eyes – panting with fear. "Aya? What is wrong?"

Aya quickly shoved the shoes back into her rucksack. "Nothing. It's OK, Mumma," she said.

"Has something happened? Has someone come for us?"

"No, Mumma, everything's good. Go back to sleep. You need to rest."

The sound of the man singing continued to float along the hallway, as Aya carefully tucked the shoes back into the bottom of her bag – along with the dreams they had briefly set dancing through the cramped little room. Then she climbed back into bed.

Chapter 4

She couldn't help going back the next day. Even though Mumma's headache was worse and Moosa was restless. Even though she needed to talk to the food-bank lady about nappies for Moosa. And ask Sally about trying to get a doctor for Mumma. Even though they still hadn't seen their new caseworker about the appeal. Even though all of that was her responsibility now…

It was the music. The tinkling tune of a piano that had danced through her head all night, and trilled through her fingers all morning. It was school holidays here, so there were dance classes going on all morning, and Aya sat on a hard plastic chair, swinging her legs in time to the music, dancing patterns on the chair leg with her fingers until she felt like she would burst if she didn't go up for another look.

"Would you be able to watch Moosa, just for a minute?"

She was sitting next to Mr Abdul – the nice old man from Somalia. The day before, Aya had taught him a few words of English and he had started showing her how to play chess. He called her his "young English professor" and shared his peppermints with her.

"I'll come straight back again," she said, speaking in the native Arabic they both shared, even though they had come from different corners of the world. "My mumma, she is—"

"She's disappearing under the waves," Mr Abdul said, glancing at Mumma, who sat on one of the sofas with her eyes closed.

"She just didn't sleep well," Aya said quickly.

"Go, go, little professor," Mr Abdul said with a smile. "I will keep an eye on the little one!" He waved a hand towards Moosa, who was playing with a box of toys that one of the volunteers had brought along.

"Thank you!" said Aya. "Thank you!"

"No need to thank me," said Mr Abdul. "We floating people need to look out for one another – or who will? Am I right, little one?"

Aya ran up the stairs, two at a time. The dance class was already in progress. It was mostly the same girls as the day before, moving through the same exercises, the thud of satin slippers on the floorboards, and the rhythmic tap of the teacher's cane and her sing-song voice echoing around the room. Aya stood by the door, breathless, watching. The blonde girl was there again. And the mousey-haired dancer with the anxious face. The tall girl. The red-head ... only the one called Dotty was missing today.

"So you are real!"

Aya spun round quickly, heat flooding to her cheeks.

"I knew it! I knew you couldn't be a ghost!"

"Ghost?"

"Yeah. I wondered if you were a fairy or something, at first." The girl called Dotty was throwing down her bag and pulling off bright-pink fluffy tracksuit bottoms and a sparkly crop top to reveal her ballet clothes underneath.

Aya glanced around nervously, suddenly unsure if she was allowed to be here.

"Then I thought you might be the ghost of some long-ago ballet student who had died in a freak pirouette accident," the girl was saying. Her skin was the colour of the sweet almonds Mumma bought in the covered market in Aleppo. "Or perhaps just keeled over from boredom in one of Miss Helena's endless barre exercises!" She acted out a dramatic swoon before quickly recovering and adopting a theatrical pose as she declared, "Destined to wander the halls of this community centre forever."

Aya glanced towards the studio door.

"Sorry – I'm Dotty, by the way." She stuck out a hand very formally, and Aya reached out her own.

"I am Aya." Her words came out awkwardly and she bit her lip. She knew she sounded foreign – different.

But the girl called Dotty didn't seem to notice. "Cool – nice name!" she declared.

She was wearing a different leotard from the one she'd worn yesterday. It had a lace insert across the back and triple straps that criss-crossed daringly over her shoulders. It was the sort of thing Samia would have liked, Aya thought. Samia, who had a different leotard for every day of the week – and two on Sundays. Samia who had lived in the apartment block round the corner from hers. Who she had gone to dance class with since they were six years old, walking along the dusty boulevard hand in hand with their ballet bags slung over their shoulders, Samia talking and talking and Aya listening and laughing.

"You do kinda look like a ghost an' all," said the girl called Dotty. She had the same thick, flat northern vowels as Sally and the other volunteer helpers in the centre, Aya noticed. She pronounced ghost like "gurst" and said look with an "oo" of surprise. "I mean, only cos you look a bit old-fashioned," Dotty went on. "If you don't mind me saying."

Aya coloured. She knew what she must look like. In trainers that were slightly too big, a skirt that was slightly too small, a boys' sweatshirt and a headscarf that looked more like a tea towel, she had become used to feeling different. At least it was better than just being invisible. But today – now – she didn't want this girl to see her like that.

"Oh, not in a bad way," Dotty went on, now attempting to tug her unruly black curls up into a lopsided ponytail. "It's just with you being so thin an' all. I mean, you can't really imagine a chubby ghost, can you?"

The words seemed to pour out of her – like bubbles, or glitter, Aya thought. That was like Samia too. Samia's family had left just before Aya's. Perhaps they were in the UK now as well. Or Germany. Or France. Or maybe still in one of the refugee camps along the way.

If they had made it out at all.

"OK, so if you're not a ghost, I'm guessing you're from the place downstairs?" Dotty was ready now, but stood, hands on hips, surveying Aya, as if she were an exotic species of butterfly or a particularly interesting new flavour of jelly bean.

"Yes." Aya bit her lip.

"That is pretty cool too," said Dotty with a cheerful grin. "Not quite as good as a ghost, but I've never met a refugee properly either. Where you from then?"

"Syria," said Aya quietly. "Aleppo."

"Cool – that place from the news!" Dotty looked excited. "No idea where it is though."

"Dotty Buchanan!" came a voice from inside the dance studio. "You are late. Very late!"

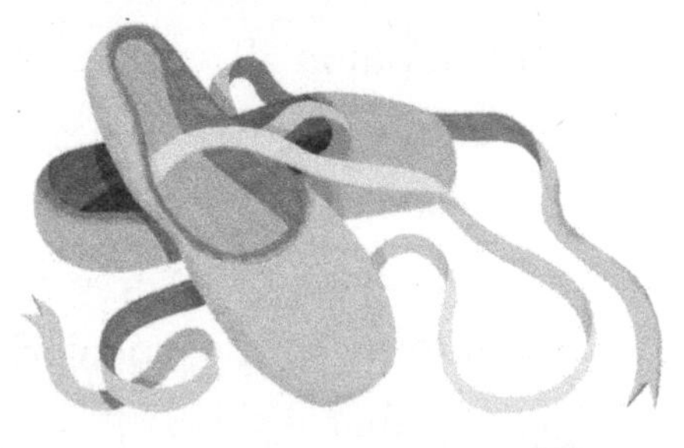

Chapter 5

Dotty shrugged and grinned. "Alas, duty calls! Nice to meet you though, Syria Girl." She paused for a second by the door, looking at Aya closely, and her expression changed suddenly. "Hey, I'm dead sorry if I said the wrong thing, by the way. I do that. My mum says I speak without thinking."

Aya shook her head. "You … didn't."

"Dotty Buchanan!" came the voice from inside the studio again. "You will please get in here."

Dotty was still watching Aya with a look of concern. "Come back – won't you?"

Aya wanted to say something, but the door to the studio was opening and there stood the dance mistress. Up close, Aya thought she looked even smaller, like a tiny, tough little fairy grandmother. She was much older than Madam Belova, but there was something about the elegance of her movement, the tilt of her chin, that reminded Aya of her old teacher – a kind of indefinable grace that shimmered around the old lady like fairy dust.

"Dotty Buchanan, what are you doing shilly and shallying out here – and so late?"

"Sorry! My mum was in rehearsal, then we got caught in traffic – and then I met Aya."

The ballet mistress glanced skirtingly in Aya's direction before tapping her watch and staring significantly at Dotty. "Time, Miss Buchanan!"

"But Aya is a refugee – from Syria," Dotty explained. "How cool is that, Miss Helena?"

Miss Helena flicked another fleeting glance in Aya's direction. This time she frowned ever so slightly.

"That is very 'cool' but I am thinking that you are the one with the big audition coming up, Miss Buchanan, so perhaps you should spend less time chittering and more time perfecting your *développés*, yes?"

"Yes, Miss Helena," Dotty sighed, glancing apologetically at Aya as she started to make her way into the studio. Then she stopped by the doorway. "Hey, could Aya join our class?"

Aya felt as if a swarm of butterflies had suddenly awoken within her belly, coloured wings fluttering.

"I mean, look at the way she stands," Dotty was saying. "It's dead obvious she's a dancer."

"This class, it is full," said Miss Helena gently but firmly.

"But—" Dotty cut in.

The butterfly wings scattered like fallen leaves in Aya's empty belly. For some reason she felt like crying. And she hadn't allowed herself to cry for weeks.

"But nothing, Dotty Buchanan," said Miss Helena sharply, though she glanced at Aya again, an odd expression in her eyes. "Let us be getting to the barre!"

Aya blinked hard and tipped her chin up firmly. She hadn't cried since Dad and she wouldn't let herself do it now.

"You *will* come back again!" Dotty whispered as Miss Helena hustled her into the classroom.

"I don't know," Aya heard herself say. "I can try."

"Promise?" said Dotty.

Aya thought of all the promises she had made. To Mumma, to Moosa, to Dad.

Miss Helena was shooing Dotty into the room. She looked back and Aya nodded – ever so slightly.

"OK. I promise."

Aleppo, Syria

The war came to Aleppo just after Aya's seventh birthday. Mumma had made the traditional tabouleh, *and an almond cake with a ballerina on the top, and she had invited all the girls from her dance class to a sleepover. The evening was so mild that Mumma said they could sleep out on the roof terrace, under the stars.*

Samia was dancing around, doing impressions of her favourite pop star. Nadiya and Nooda were making up a routine that looked as if they were one girl, dancing in front of a mirror. Kimi was drawing pictures of ballerinas in pink and lilac and turquoise tutus. There had been music coming from the garden below and the smell of Mumma cooking mahashi *in the kitchen.*

When the first explosions happened, Aya had thought they were fireworks going off in the eastern part of the city. Fireworks for her birthday.

But Dad came home early from the hospital and she heard him and her mother talking in low, urgent voices in the kitchen. "Protestors shot by government troops … fighting in the Old City," she heard him say. The beautiful old covered market where Mumma had bought fruit and almonds for Aya's birthday cake had been damaged, bullet holes pock-marking the walls of the ancient suk.

Mumma gathered all the girls inside. It was not safe to sleep on the roof, she said, so they made a den of mattresses in Aya's room and lit the candles on the cake and sang Happy Birthday. But the evening was spoiled somehow, and Aya could not fall asleep for a long time because of the sound of gunfire.

The following day they found out that Samia's older brother Rami had been to the protest. He'd been one of the lucky ones. He came home with just scratches and a frightened look in his eyes. Others had not been so fortunate.

Over the next few days the fighting got more intense. The eastern part of the city was taken by the rebels and Aleppo felt as if it had been cut in half. Now there were soldiers patrolling the streets near Aya's home, and Dad said they could not go to the western part of Aleppo because it was occupied by government troops. Luckily Madam Belova's dance studio was in their quarter of the city – that was all that mattered to Aya back then.

The party gifts were all packed away, the last of the cake eaten, but the sound of gunfire did not stop. It was surprising how quickly something like that started to feel … normal.

Chapter 6

"My father is a doctor," Aya explained, for what felt like the millionth time. "I mean – he was."

This was a new caseworker. Not the one they had seen in the detention centre in Bedford. He didn't seem to have their files. They had been lost or mislaid somewhere – nobody seemed to know where – when they had been moved out of the centre and relocated to Manchester, and so Aya had to go over everything all over again.

"He worked in a hospital in Aleppo, but before that he was in England for five years – in a place called Birm-ing-ham." Aya sounded out the unfamiliar name, remembering how Dad had always pronounced it with a funny nasal accent that had made her laugh. "He had papers from the hospital there. They say they will find him a job."

"Do you still have the papers?" The young caseworker looked up hopefully. He was in his early twenties, with a smattering of a beard growing across his face. He looked very tired.

Aya shook her head. "They were—" she hesitated "—also lost."

Moosa was attempting to clamber under one of the tables by the food bank, and the two elderly ladies in charge were looking cross. Aya went to rescue him before he bashed his head or knocked something over.

"Enough mischief, Moosa!" she said, feeling tired. "Aya is trying to sort things out, so she needs you to be good today, OK?"

The young caseworker was looking impatient as Aya returned with a wriggling Moosa in her arms. Mumma was fiddling with her sleeve, the way she did when she was upset or anxious. Aya leaned over and stroked her hand. "Don't worry, Mumma. It's going to be fine."

"And your initial claim for asylum was rejected because…?" The caseworker was asking questions again. Aya wanted to ask why they had been moved here, and why she had to go over all this stuff again. There never seemed to be time to ask those things.

"I don't know. They say we are entering the country illegally," said Aya.

She remembered the immigration officials, bundling them all into the back of a police van and taking them to the detention centre, which felt more like a prison than a place of safe haven.

"And I think the other lady – our caseworker before – she said we had already claimed safe haven in Turkey ... or Greece, I think – and so we cannot apply for asylum here." These words had become familiar to Aya now – "safe haven", "asylum", "refugee status", "right to remain". She knew the words even though she still didn't fully understand what they meant.

"I see." The young man sifted through papers with a frown as Moosa wriggled his way off Aya's lap again. "Well, I'll see what I can do."

"But we hadn't," said Aya quickly, as Moosa tottered off in the direction of the food bank again. "You see, they interviewed my mother. When we first arrived in the detention centre – three weeks ago."

Three weeks. Had they really only been in England for less than a month?

"But she wasn't very well. And her English..."

She wanted to explain. About how things had been after Dad. About the refugee camp … and Mumma being unwell. About the caseworker at the detention centre who had insisted on interviewing her without Aya – how Mumma probably hadn't understood what they had been asking her.

But the young man had already started putting away papers in the folder and didn't seem to be listening any more. Moosa was being shooed away from the piles of tins and packages by the two fierce-looking ladies, who were tutting crossly.

"I understand." He removed his glasses and rubbed his temples, and Aya thought he didn't look as if he understood at all.

"But we can apply again? We can appeal?" asked Aya. "The other caseworker – she said we could appeal?"

"I'll look into it," said the tired young man, scribbling something on a piece of paper. "Now I must see the next person."

Moosa had fallen over and bumped his head. He was crying now, a high-pitched wail that made Aya feel suddenly desperate.

"They won't send us back, will they?"

The caseworker was beckoning to the next family and Aya could feel panic rising. She had waited so long to talk to him and there were so many things she still needed to ask.

"Ay-a… Ay-a!" Moosa's sobs rose high in the hot air.

"They can't – can they?" Aya demanded. "They can't send us back to Aleppo?"

She remembered what Mr Abdul had called them – "floating people". Sometimes it felt like they were pieces of driftwood, forever being moved on the ebb and flow of the tide, with no choice where they were taken – always at the mercy of others.

"I will do my very best."

And then the caseworker was opening the next file and Moosa was red-faced and whimpering in the arms of one of the food-bank ladies, who was tutting crossly and saying something about keeping children under control. He reached out his little fingers towards Aya and murmured, "Dada, want Dada!"

"Me too, Moos!" said Aya as she reached out a finger to Moosa's outstretched palm and took his tiny sticky hand in her own. "Me too!"

Chapter 7

It took ages to calm Moosa. Aya bounced him up and down on her hip, crooning quietly, trying to remember the song Dad used to sing when she couldn't get to sleep. Or when there was a storm. Or the first night the bombs fell. The song about sunshine after rain and grey clouds with silver linings. But she couldn't remember all the words. And it didn't work anyway.

"Want Dada!" Moosa wailed again.

"Hush, Moosie. Everything's going to be OK," she said, kissing the tears off his hot little cheeks and humming bits of the tune into his damp hair. That's what Dad had always said – that everything would be OK when they got to England. But now they were here and it wasn't … and he wasn't with them … and Aya felt so tired and so angry suddenly. Because it wasn't fair! It wasn't fair that Dad was gone and Mumma was sick and she was supposed to sort everything out. Always being moved and not knowing why. It wasn't fair that she had to look after Moosa and he always needed something – someone. She felt as if she might explode. It wasn't fair! None of it was fair!

Moosa fell asleep eventually, exhausted, his eyelashes still damp with tears as Aya laid him down in the buggy. The music had started upstairs again and today it seemed to tug at the ball of anger inside her, pulling strands of it free – the bombs, the camp, the border guards, the container, the sea… All the memories she tried so hard to keep locked away.

"You OK, little professor?" asked Mr Abdul with his big white-teeth smile. "You want to play some chess?"

"Not right now. I'm just … going out," she said. "I need some air."

Aya pushed her way out through the fire door at the back of the hall and found herself in a small concrete yard, closed in by red-brick walls on three sides, and rusting wire meshing on the fourth. A square of white Manchester sky above. Weeds growing through black crazy paving below. Cigarette butts strewn in a corner by the wheelie bins. The smell of refuse and exhaust fumes and hot soup from the kitchen.

The music was louder out here. And the piece that was playing was familiar, though Aya could not think where she'd heard it before. The notes seemed to fly around – like shrapnel, like falling rubble from bombed buildings, like swirling dust on the streets of her home after the first shells fell.

A memory of sunny Syrian skies, of running to her old dance studio past Bab-al-Nasr, the Victory Gate, laughing as she made her way up the stairs to the studio with her classmates. Samia making a joke about a boy from school…

The notes rippled across her like pebbles skimming across the sea, running through her fingers, her toes. Aya ran a few steps across the concrete, stopped by the railings, feeling her body twist into a pirouette.

Sitting on the roof of their apartment on a summer's evening, watching sunset over the citadel. Dad playing the harmonica while Aya and Moosa spun round and round and round and Mumma laughed, her hands covered in flour…

She stopped and closed her eyes. Holding on tight to the memories that spilled out and threatened to spill her with them, as she rose to *demi-pointe*, extending her leg in a sweeping movement.

The girls in the dance studio, laughing before class, pulling on ballet shoes… Samia telling a silly story that made everyone laugh, even the twins who were usually so serious…

Madam Belova leaning on the windowsill with her sardonic smile as she watched them warm up…

Aya pushed off against the wall, up on her toes now, then spinning into a pirouette. She felt as if something inside her was coming loose and it hurt – but it also felt good.

The bombs falling – the ruins of Bab-al-Nasr and the old suk – the sight of the dance studio now a skeleton – barres hanging off the walls, mirrors shattered by the blast. Dad saying they had to run…

Aya let the emotions take her now. The music sped up and she leapt, air-bound, hands shooting upwards towards the white sky, then plummeting low to the weed-strewn ground.

The memories rushed in … border guards … the refugee camp … the airless container … the boat across the sea … the storm…

She spun again – one, two, three times.

The sea … the boat … the beach … blood in the water…

Her body jerked to a stop. No – there were things she couldn't allow herself to remember.

"Sometimes the only thing you can do is dance, isn't it?"

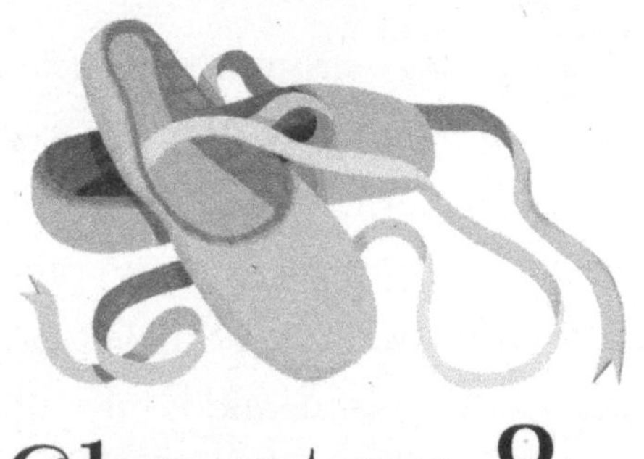

Chapter 8

Aya lurched back into the present. She felt dizzy and dazed, and it took her a second to reconnect with where she was.

Standing at the top of the metal fire escape was the tiny old dance teacher. Today she was dressed in a long purple skirt and giant grey knitted cardigan that swept nearly to her ankles. She looked even more like an ancient fairy queen – skin papery, eyes two violets, hair like thistledown.

"You feel the music in here." The old lady tapped her own chest as she made her way carefully down the metal staircase, watching Aya intently.

Aya was breathless and dizzy, still taking in the red-brick walls, the wheelie bins, the rusted railing... For a few moments she'd been back in Aleppo.

"I saw you watching my class the other day."

Aya felt herself stiffen. "I'm sorry – I—"

The old lady waved her hand dismissively. "You have been trained where?"

"Trained?" She realised she'd become used to mistrusting people – it was a hard habit to break. The old lady was looking her up and down with a critical, appraising eye that made Aya feel stiff and self-conscious.

"Which ballet school do you go to?"

"I – don't. We've only just arrived. In England. Three weeks."

"Three weeks. And before that?"

Aya thought of the list of places they had travelled through. She remembered Dad counting them off on his long brown fingers and laughing: Syria, the camp at Kilis, across the sea from Izmir, to Greece – the beach on Chios – all the way to England. "Our Grand Tour," he had called it. Only Dad could have made fleeing their home seem like an adventure.

"Aleppo," Aya said quietly.

"I see." The old lady seemed to comprehend something and she nodded. "Sometimes it seems that the world never learns."

The sun had come out through the white blanket of cloud, making even the dirty red brick take on a brighter hue.

"I – I do not understand."

"No, of course you don't." The old lady's eyes traced Aya's features, and for the second time in two days, she felt that somebody was really looking *at* her – not through her.

"Perhaps," said the old lady quietly, "you would be liking to join my dance class upstairs?"

Aya felt herself flush. "You said there is no space…"

"For the right dancers, we can always find a little more space, I think."

Hot steam belched out of a pipe, giving off a smell of stewed meat and carrots. Aya's stomach rumbled and she realised how hungry she was. She looked down at her feet and shrugged. "I … we have no money – to pay. For the lessons."

The old lady moved slowly down the last few steps, her eyes intently on Aya.

"When I first came to England," she said, glancing around at the weeds and the cigarette butts, "I relied a great deal on the kindness of strangers – as somebody once said. I forget who."

The concrete slabs beneath Aya's feet felt rough and

the sun beat down, hot and sticky. A pulse was beating hard in her tummy. She needed to check Moosa was OK. Get him something to eat. And Mumma too. Yesterday she had barely eaten anything.

"Sometimes we need to let ourselves accept help from others." The old lady reached into her pocket and unwrapped a bar of dark chocolate, breaking off a piece and handing it to Aya before popping a square in her own mouth.

Aya took a bite. The chocolate was rich and bitter, with a tang of something sweet – cherry or orange.

"Perhaps I can have a word with your parents? About the dancing."

"There is only – my mumma." She felt as if the words might trip her so she trod carefully over them, like stepping stones. "She does not speak English."

From somewhere, not far away, she could hear a siren going off and the sound of traffic.

"Maybe we can speak to your *maminka* together then."

Into Aya's brain flashed an image of Madam Belova. Her neat blonde bob, dark penetrating eyes, the curve of her mouth when she saw a movement she liked. She had a feeling Madam Belova and this old lady would have got on.

"Please, Madam, I—" Aya began to say.

The old lady stopped her. "No Madam here. I am Miss Helena. And you are…?" Her milky-blue eyes twinkled as Aya looked up to meet them.

"Aya."

"Well, Miss Aya from Aleppo." Miss Helena smiled. "I think you must come and see what you think of our little dance class?"

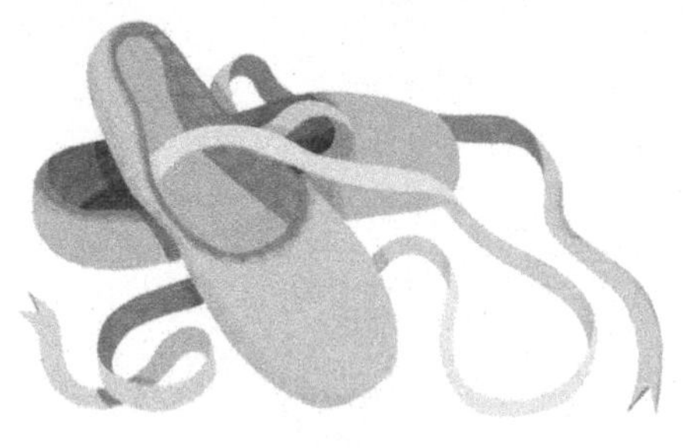

Chapter 9

The lesson had started by the time they got up to the studio. Another teacher stood by the barre. She was maybe thirty years younger than Miss Helena, and taller too, but with the same bright-blue eyes and erect carriage, her steel-grey hair cut in a severe bob. The music was playing and the girls were doing a very fast exercise at the barre – a *battement frappé* – their feet darting back and forth in double time, their heads moving in unison – but all eyes swivelled to follow Aya as Miss Helena ushered her into the room.

"Eyes front," Miss Helena said as she crossed to the barre. "Chins up. No, no, no, Dotty! This is the corps de ballet, not the dance of the corpses! You must be looking enchanted … not like a – how do you say it? A zom-bie!"

The girls giggled as Dotty pulled a zombie face then, as the exercise came to an end, turned to look curiously at Aya, who stood awkwardly by the door. Dotty's face broke into a huge grin.

"Hi, ghost-girl!" she mouthed.

Miss Helena was introducing Aya to the younger teacher. "This is my daughter, Miss Sylvie," she said. "She is in charge of the day-to-day things at the school. This is Aya."

Miss Sylvie – who seemed too old to be described as anyone's daughter – nodded and put out her hand formally. "Pleased to meet you, Aya." She was stiffer than her mother, but her stern face was not unkind, though her expression was a little curious.

The older ballet mistress had turned to the assembled girls. "Aya will be joining class today."

"Dressed like that?" The blonde girl called Ciara was the one who spoke. She wore a leotard with a lace panel, like curling tendrils of flowers, and her skin was so white it made Aya think of coconut milk.

Aya flushed and glanced at her own reflection in the liver-spotted mirrors. She wore leggings and an old T-shirt that she had been given at the detention centre in Bedford. It was a boys' style and several sizes too big for her. Her feet were bare and dirty inside an old pair of Mumma's sandals and she felt – she searched for the word and couldn't find it. Strange? Alien? Lost? She knew that's what she must look like to these girls.

"Ciara, you might like to focus more on your own sloppy *cou-de-pied* and less on others' fashion choices," said Miss Sylvie curtly.

The small red-headed girl giggled, and even the tall, anxious girl with glasses twisted her mouth into a smile. Dotty let out a loud snort.

"But you said the class was full—" Ciara objected.

"Then let us hope one of you is not asked to leave!" said Miss Helena.

Ciara went even paler and said nothing more, but her eyes flashed crossly in Aya's direction.

"And now – if no one has any objections –" Miss Helena raised her eyebrows – "We will begin!"

Aya wanted to run away suddenly. To say that she couldn't stay long. That she had to get back to Moosa – and Mumma. But the music had begun and the other girls were moving, and she had no choice but to join them.

It was a simple barre exercise, the sort of thing Aya had done a million times at Madam Belova's. But that felt like a lifetime ago.

Dotty turned to her and whispered, "Copy me. Well, the steps, anyway. Don't copy my technique or you'll be in all sorts of trouble!"

Aya felt a wave of gratitude along with a welling sense of panic. What if the music made her feel like it had earlier? When all the memories had spilled out of her – out of control…?

She tried hard to think only about the steps, blocking everything else out and focusing only on the gentle rhythmic shuffle and thud of satin feet on the floor, the hum of the air conditioning, the smell of sweat and rosin, helping her feet and arms find the old familiar shapes.

"Bottoms in, ladies!" Miss Helena was saying. "Dotty – are you remembering the twenty-pound note? You have a twenty-pound note held tight between the cheeks of your bottom. You do not want to lose it, so you must clench – tight – so!"

Aya smiled. Madam Belova had said once that the body held on to memories – in the arms, the legs, the toes, the fingertips. Muscle memory, she called it. And as the music flowed and they moved through each different exercise, Aya felt her body remember. From the smooth elasticity of *battement fondu* to the rapid *battement frappé*, the slow and sustained *relevé lent* to the fast, sweeping *grand battement*, Aya felt each movement release memories that had been locked tight in her muscles. It felt painful and hard but beautifully bitter-sweet. Magical.

"Very nice," Miss Helena was saying. Aya had barely realised the music had come to an end. The other girls were smiling, and – with a shock – Aya realised the teacher had been talking to her.

Aleppo, Syria

The day she realised the war had really come to Aleppo, Aya had been at a dance lesson. Madam Belova had been teaching them how to do an arabesque. Just a very simple arabesque parterre *– that was what you had to master before attempting to lift your leg, Madam had said. Still, Aya remembered how she had felt like a fairy, like a bird about to take flight.*

"Your arms must be extended in harmony with your legs," Madam was saying. "To form a graceful curve from fingertips to toes—"

The explosion shook the building like an earthquake. The lights went out and dust fell from the ceiling. One of the mirrors cracked.

Aya remembered the silence afterwards – louder even than the noise of the explosion. It seemed to go on forever. Then the sound of sirens wailing. Everyone coughing. Madam Belova calling,

"Girls – are you OK? Is everyone all right?" And then – weirdly – the music starting again – the CD player picking up where it had left off, barely missing a beat. As if nothing had happened. As if the world hadn't changed forever.

The bomb hit some apartment blocks near the hospital where Dad worked. And the thousand-year-old minaret of the Umayyad Mosque was also hit. Many worshippers had been trapped inside when it collapsed. Later that evening, Aya heard Dad talking to Mumma about the casualties who had been brought to the hospital. There had been terrible, terrible injuries, he said.

"A thousand years it has been standing," she heard Dad say. "And then in one day – destroyed, and so many lives with it."

Aya was in the sitting room, practising her arabesque croisé. *Dad and Mumma were in the kitchen, sitting in the dark with only candles for light because there had been a power cut.*

"The radio says troops have cut off the main highway to the south," Mumma said. "People are saying that there will be a siege."

Aya looked up. She didn't know what the word meant. Not then.

"But if there is a siege, what will we do?"

There was a silence. Aya imagined her father going to stand behind Mumma, rubbing her temples the way she liked when she got one of her headaches.

"We will cope," she heard him say.

Aya lifted her head as Madam Belova had taught her, keeping her back strong and square, and trying to follow the line of her arm with her eyes.

"It cannot last forever," Dad was saying.

Very, very carefully, Aya lifted her leg, trying to visualise the shape she wanted to make, keeping the line exactly. It was easier somehow in the dark. Mumma was saying something that Aya couldn't make out. Aya lifted her tummy and felt the lovely curved line rippling through her whole body – just for a second.

"Things must be resolved eventually," Dad said. "One way or another."

She wobbled then and lost the shape but she could remember what it felt like and she knew she would be able to find it again next time.

Chapter 10

The lesson seemed to go by in a heartbeat for Aya. Concentrating on the dance steps. Sinking back into remembered movements, letting go – just for a short while. Allowing herself to forget about Moosa and Mumma – and Dad. It felt so good, too good – and it went too fast. Before she knew it, it was over and Aya felt light and a bit strange, and guilty – but in a good way.

As the other girls took their curtseys and began to make their way out, Dotty grabbed Aya and dragged her out into the lobby, grinning broadly.

"I've been telling everyone all about you," she said with a grin. "They thought you were a figment of my overactive imagination! Like the time I thought I saw a tarantula in the toilets that turned out to just be a mop head…"

Dotty performed a little dance – her body and her face transformed first into a spider, then into a mop sweeping the floor.

"Or the time you told us the man in the corner shop was a vampire," said the girl called Lilli-Ella, rolling her eyes.

"Yeah, well, I still reckon he's got the look of the undead about him!" said Dotty, and this time she did a turn as some sort of zombie vampire that made all the other girls giggle. She was a natural performer, Aya thought, as Dotty collapsed in an undead heap on the floor.

"Anyway, the fact is, I didn't make Aya up!" said Dotty, sitting up and grinning. "I mean, even I couldn't imagine someone who dances like she does!"

"What's so special about the way she dances?"

"I am going to ignore that comment, Ciara," said Dotty. "Cos clearly you've taken a blow to the head, or need a guide dog or summat, or you wouldn't have asked."

Aya glanced at Ciara, who was eyeing her with suspicion. She felt herself flush.

"OK, so the charming Ciara clearly needs no

introduction. Now you'd better meet the rest of the gang," Dotty went on. "This is Lilli-Ella. She's only in Year Five and she's already in the advanced class with us ancient Year Sixes, so she's basically a child prodigy."

"I am so not!" Lilli-Ella smiled and blushed. "But it's nice to meet you, Aya."

Aya nodded and tried to smile.

"And this is Grace," Dotty went on. "She's far too nice for her own good!"

The tall girl stooped to shake hands very formally with Aya, her eyes blinking nervously. "Actually, I'm the class giraffe," she said. "All long limbs and no grace – which makes my name ironic, I know!"

Aya felt Grace's hand warmly grip her own. She reminded her of Assia, who had been in her class at school. She came top in every science test but tripped up over her own feet in basketball. Assia's family had left Aleppo before the siege. Fled overnight. One day Aya had turned up at school and Assia's desk was empty. Gone – just like that. They had gone to Germany, Aya found out later. They had family there. She hadn't heard from her again.

"And this is Blue," Dotty went on. "The most colourful member of the class!"

Blue grinned. "I know – it's a dumb name. And it's doubly confusing because of the hair." She held up a strand of copper-coloured hair and sighed. "My parents were – well, I don't know what they were thinking!"

"You should be called Red," Dotty chipped in helpfully. "Or perhaps Ginger – good name for a dancer! Not a ballet dancer, mind you. Far too cool for ballet!"

"Basically, I suit my name about as well as Grace suits hers!" said Blue with an expressive shrug.

"On the other hand, people are always telling me how much my name becomes me," Dotty was saying. She had let her corkscrew hair out of the tight ponytail, so that it fluffed out around her head like a halo.

"You know, cos it means scatty, forgetful, bonkers." Dotty did a series of head-twirling and hand-spinning gestures to make her point, and Aya found herself smiling.

"So you learned to dance where you came from?" Aya looked up to see Ciara was watching her intently from the other side of the lobby.

"She's come from Syria, not from Mars!" said Dotty.

"I thought they had a war in Syria," said Ciara.

The girls were all looking at her curiously now and

Aya wanted to explain that her life had been like theirs once. That she hadn't been born a refugee. That she wasn't so different from them. Or she hadn't been. Once upon a time. But all she managed to say was, "It was not always that way."

She thought of her old classmates – scattered, lost, gone – while these girls danced on, knowing nothing of the war happening in a country far away, and staring at her curiously, seeing her as different.

"Shoo, shoo, shoo!" Madam Sylvie was at the door, waving the girls away. "Don't you have homes to go to?"

The girls jumped up, grabbing bags and shoes and collecting lost bobbles and hairpins that had scattered across the floor.

"See you tomorrow, Aya!" called out little Lilli-Ella. A chorus of other farewells followed as her new classmates made their way down the stairs.

"Oops! Gotta dash!" said Dotty, leaping to her feet and following them. "But I'll bring you a leotard tomorrow, OK?"

Aya wanted to beg her not to but the words did not come. And then they were gone – and she was alone again, standing in the lobby, the phrase "Don't you have homes to go to?" bouncing in her mind.

Such a simple question. But she didn't have an answer. She moved her foot in a slow circle across the floor, then made her way back downstairs.

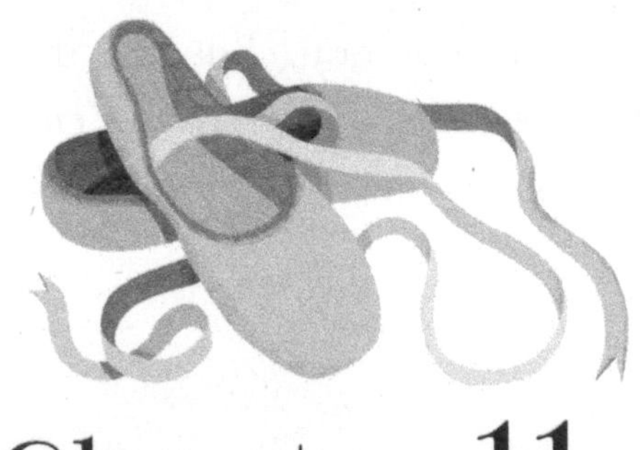

Chapter 11

Sometimes, at night, Aya dreamed of dancing in Syria again. Usually she was dancing on the rooftop garden of their old apartment block. Or at the Maysaloon Park where Dad used to take her on Sunday afternoons, particularly after Mumma fell pregnant and needed "a bit of peace and quiet". Or in Madam Belova's studio, sand beneath the satin and burlap of her pointe shoes. She always woke with an ache, as if she were remembering a missing arm or leg … something vitally part of her that was now gone.

But that night she dreamed of dancing in Miss Helena's dance studio and she awoke with a smile on her face for the first time in … she didn't know how long.

The feeling didn't last. Moosa had a snotty nose and his bottom was sore because they had run out of nappies. He was grizzling and whining unhappily as she tried to get him dressed.

"We'll get you some new nappies, Moos," she said. She was trying to talk to him in English as much as she could, teaching him as Dad had taught her. "And some cream for your bottom too. Aya's gonna make it all better, OK?" She kissed him on his pink, snotty nose and he sniffed and gazed at her with big, damp eyes that made her heart want to break.

"Bet-ter," he muttered in English.

"All better!" said Aya, kissing him again. "Promise!"

But when she came downstairs there was a problem. The man who ran the hostel was shouting at Mumma, who was crying, confused, not understanding what he was saying. And the man was waving his arms aggressively, pointing at a piece of paper – stabbing it in front of her face.

"My mother cannot talk English," Aya explained, stepping in between them and taking the paper from the hostel owner. "Please tell me."

"The room's not been paid for. No rent, no room," said the man, looking Aya up and down with that look in his eyes that she'd seen before. Worse than being invisible. Like she was a nuisance, a burden, an outsider.

She tried to remember what the caseworker had said. About papers and welfare payments and housing benefit – words she hadn't really understood.

"Our papers … are getting lost," she tried to explain. "And my mumma has been ill."

"Look, I'm not interested in sob stories. I need money by the end of the week or you are out."

The man was balding, with a red face and a stained T-shirt that didn't quite stretch over his belly. He reminded Aya of the horrible maths teacher who had come to cover for them after Mr Attia got caught up in the demonstrations and stopped coming to school – the one Samia had said had an alien growing in his stomach.

"But you cannot do that," Aya said, her face screwed into a frown. She tried to sound like she knew what she was talking about, even though she had no idea. "We have nowhere else to go."

"Not my problem! I'm sick of you refugees coming here and taking advantage. Sort it out or find somewhere else to stay." He turned away, shaking his head in disgust.

Aya didn't translate the last bit for her mother. Instead, she tried to imagine an alien crawling its way out of the man's belly and eating him all up – just like the picture Samia had drawn of the awful maths teacher. Somehow, today it didn't make her feel much better. And the warm, happy feeling she had woken up with was gone too.

"Come on," she said, hoiking Moosa up on to her hip where he stopped grizzling immediately. "We will leave the nasty man and go and see Mr Abdul, eh? And Mrs Massoud – and nice Sally who said you looked like her nephew and gave you the little cake. Maybe she will have another treat for you, Moosie?"

Moosa giggled and grabbed at her hair, twisting it round his fingers.

She turned and took her mother gently by the arm. Her face was red and blotchy and her eyes looked so tired this morning.

"You are a good girl, Aya," Mumma said, patting Aya's hand absently.

"I'm going to talk to someone at the centre," said Aya. "Sally – or the caseworker man. About the rent and the papers. They will be able to help. Sort this all out. Everything will be fine, I promise."

Chapter 12

But five hours later she was still sitting in the community centre, watching as the clock on the wall ticked towards one o'clock. They still hadn't seen the man who Sally had said might be able to give them advice on housing, and there was no sign of Miss Helena either.

"How long you think we spend sitting in queue like this, Miss Aya-My-Professor?" asked Mr Abdul. He needed to talk to someone about medicine for his arthritis, but nobody seemed to know quite who he was supposed to speak to. The whole centre was run by volunteers, and there were always too many people, too many problems – not enough time.

"Weeks and weeks," said Aya with a smile.

"And months ... and years..." Mr Abdul sing-songed.

"Lifetimes!" said Aya, and they both laughed.

"Queuing and queuing – filling in forms and answering questions," said Mr Abdul in his deep, throaty, sing-along voice. "Waiting, asking for help, answering the same questions over and over again..."

"I can maybe help you translate," Aya said. "If you need me to. Sally said the translator cannot come today."

"Thank you, little professor," said Mr Abdul – his old face lighting up with the big smile that came out like sun from behind a rain cloud. "And the words you teach me are up here!" He tapped the white fuzz on top of his head. "My English will be so nice – soon I will not need translator!" He grinned and added, "Thanking you *ve-ry* much!" in his best English, before finishing with a throaty laugh.

"But still – if you want. I can try. My father taught me..."

Aya tailed off, pushing away an unbidden memory of her father – of laughing over funny-sounding English words at the kitchen table. She glanced up at the clock on the wall. Twelve fifty-five. Miss Helena had said she would talk to Mumma before the lesson, and there was no sign of her.

She's probably forgotten, thought Aya. Sometimes she felt like all the bits of lost paperwork – misplaced, forgotten, scattered along the way.

Mumma sat on a collapsing sofa in the corner while Moosa played with a small pile of toys that had been donated to the centre by some of the volunteers. Mumma seemed a little better since Aya had persuaded her to eat some breakfast but she still looked so small and faded.

"I thought I would find you here!"

Aya looked up to see Miss Helena. She wore a snowy-grey cardigan today, over a tie-dyed dress the colour of butterfly wings. Her arrival had caused a stir of interest. Mr Abdul stood and extended his hand with a small bow. "Allow me to be introduced to your friend, Miss Aya?" he said with exaggerated courtesy.

"This is Miss Helena – the dance teacher from upstairs," said Aya in Arabic. Then she switched to English. "Miss Helena, this is my friend Mr Abdul."

"A pleasure to meet you," said Mr Abdul in Arabic, taking the hand Miss Helena extended to him and kissing it chivalrously. Then he added in English, just for good measure, "Hel-lo very much!"

"He says he is pleased to meet you," Aya explained.

"I thought as much," said Miss Helena, holding Mr

Abdul's twinkling gaze with a smile. "Please convey my pleasure in meeting him also."

Aya did so, and Mr Abdul continued to hold Miss Helena's hand a little longer than Aya felt was strictly necessary.

"And these are my friends Mr and Mrs Massoud."

"A friend of Aya is a friend of ours also," said Mrs Massoud, greeting Miss Helena with a small curtsey.

Aya introduced a couple of other centre regulars, as well as Sally, the perpetually smiling volunteer coordinator who ran the drop-in centre, and the two strict-looking food-bank ladies who had been concerned about Moosa since his bumped head the day before.

"She looks after her brother so well," said one.

"Such a good girl," said the other.

"And your *maminka*?" said Miss Helena, after all the introductions were done. "Can I meet her also?"

Aya led the dance teacher over to the sofa where her mother sat. Mumma looked startled as Miss Helena reached down and extended her hand.

"Mumma, this is Miss Helena." Aya looked at her nervously. She didn't want Mumma to get upset, and all sorts of things unsettled her these days. "She runs the dance school upstairs."

Mumma shot an anxious look at Aya.

"Please tell your mother I am very pleased to meet her," said Miss Helena gently.

Aya translated quickly and her mother nodded, but the crease in her forehead remained and she looked wary. Aya tried to remember when that wariness had crept into her mother's eyes. Was it during the siege? Or afterwards, at the refugee camp? Or not till later, after Dad...?

Moosa had clambered off the sofa and tripped up over the bag of papers that Mrs Massoud carried around everywhere. Papers to do with her missing son, Jimi, who she said she would never stop looking for. Mumma went to scoop him up, apologising in Arabic.

"Miss Helena says I can join her ballet class," Aya managed to say. She watched her mother expectantly, trying not to let herself hope too much.

"We have no money to pay for dance lessons," said Mumma in a stiff voice, bundling a wriggling Moosa up into her arms and shooting another anxious glance at Aya. "No money."

Miss Helena did not wait for Aya to translate the answer. "Perhaps you can explain that I would not expect payment."

Aya translated, aware that everyone else in the

waiting room was trying to follow the exchange with interest.

"I am thinking that Aya might assist with some of the classes for younger girls," Miss Helena went on. "Dotty helps but sometimes but she is more of an entertainer than a demonstrator!"

"A – demonstrator?" Aya didn't recognise the word in English.

"A helper," Miss Helena said with a smile. "We then will be – how do you say it – doing each other a favour!"

Aya explained this to her mother and for a moment – just for a moment – Mumma looked like her old self. Like the pretty, sweet young mother who had been left behind in Aleppo. Who applauded every new move and laughed as Aya danced around the kitchen.

Aya was looking at Mumma, her heart thumping in her chest. Mumma was facing Miss Helena and a look seemed to pass between the two women. When she turned back to Aya there were tears in her eyes as she took Aya's hand and stroked it gently between her own. "You must go, *habibti.*"

Habibti. It was Dad's word for her. Beloved, it meant. My beloved.

Aya tried to read the look in her eyes. "But don't you need me?"

"I can manage." she said quietly.

Moosa had wriggled free and was making his way towards Mrs Massoud's bag of papers again.

"But Moosa...?"

"Will survive without his big sister for an hour or two each day," said Mrs Massoud, scooping up Moosa and landing a kiss on his damp curls.

"We old ones can watch him," said Mr Abdul, as Moosa wriggled like a fish and squawked like a baby dinosaur. "How much trouble can he be?"

Sally laughed. "I'm sure we can all help," she said.

Aya glanced at Mumma. Her eyes were bright and a little misty, but Aya could not read the expression in them. "Are you sure you are OK?"

"Go," said Mumma quietly. She smiled, and for a second it was the smile that Aya remembered, with no wariness – the soft smile that reminded Aya of home. Of the smell of *manoushi* – the sweet bread Mumma used to bake on Sunday mornings. Of the sunlight falling through the skylight in the kitchen, of the sound of the radio playing, and her father calling her his dancing girl.

"Go and dance, Aya."

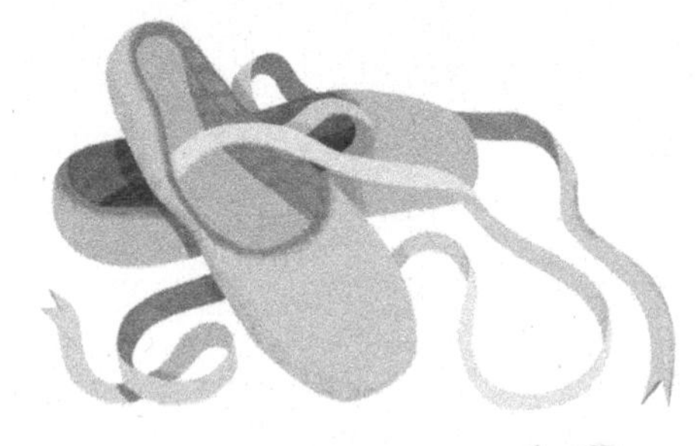

Chapter 13

Aya ran up the steps, taking them two at time, nearly colliding with Ciara at the top.

"Watch where you're going, refugee girl!"

Aya felt her bubble of excitement pop and her stomach lurched. The other girls were there too – all except Dotty – but their smiles faded on their faces and they looked at each other awkwardly, not quite meeting her eye. It was as if that word – refugee – changed the way they saw her somehow.

Ciara said it like it was an insult, just as the landlord had. *Refugee.* Aya thought of Mrs Massoud, who had lost her son and her daughter. And Mr Abdul, who told her he had fled his home with nothing when soldiers came and burned his village. They were refugees too.

She wanted to say something to make them see her normally again – to say that she was just a girl like they were, that she didn't choose for her life to be turned upside down, but the words didn't come.

"You're here!"

Dotty was sprinting up the stairs, breathless and grinning. "And I'm actually not late for once. Here – these are for you." She shoved a pile of clothes into Aya's hands – three leotards that looked hardly worn and three immaculate pairs of ballet socks.

Aya's stomach contracted again and she felt heat flood to her face.

"They don't fit me any more," Dotty was saying. "And you're much diddier than me!"

Ciara was smirking now, and the other girls were busying themselves tying shoes and fiddling with their hair. Aya knew that Dotty was trying to be nice, and the leotards were beautiful, but somehow they were worse than Ciara's insult. They made her feel like a charity case – a poor little refugee.

"Thank you," she said quietly, her face burning red.

Dotty didn't seem to be aware of her discomfort. "Come on – get changed or you'll be late, and Miss Sylvie is taking warm-up!"

But Aya took her time getting ready. She took the

beautiful leotards into the toilet and locked herself into a cubicle. By the time she re-emerged the others were already in the studio. The tight ball of anxiety in her stomach was making her feel sick.

"What *are* you wearing?"

She could hear Ciara giggling. Feel the other girls staring now. Her face burned but she did not look up.

Miss Sylvie raised her eyebrows. "No leggings in class, please. Take them off."

"I..." The knot tightened in Aya's stomach. She thought she might be sick, but still she kept her eyes down.

"You need bare legs or tights so that I can see your muscles working correctly," Miss Sylvie explained.

Aya felt blank as she sat on the bare floor and slowly peeled off the leggings. She didn't look up or say a word as she pulled off the right leg, then hesitated slightly before exposing the flesh of her left calf.

She heard Lilli-Ella gasp and Ciara make a sound between a hiccup and a giggle. Aya bit her lip to hold back the tears that she could feel beginning to form on her eyelashes. She would not cry. She would not let any of them see her cry. Especially not Ciara.

The livid scar ran right down the back of her left calf. Purple and blue, it criss-crossed her muscle like an angry river; ugly, disfiguring. She turned away her eyes so she didn't have to look at it.

Miss Sylvie took a step towards her. Aya did not look up, could not catch her eye.

"I see," said Miss Sylvie. "You should have said. Shrapnel?"

Aya nodded.

Miss Sylvie bent down and took Aya's calf in her hand, expertly turning it under the scrutiny of her eye. "Is there any permanent damage?"

"I don't think so. My father..." Aya hesitated. Her stomach tightened as it always did when she said Dad's name. "He said there will be no damage – for long term."

The other girls had fallen silent. Even Ciara was no longer sniggering. But Aya knew that they were all staring. And pitying her – the refugee, the charity case, the war child, the victim...

"Perhaps you would prefer to wear tights," said Miss Sylvie.

"No!" The bell-like voice of Miss Helena rang out, and the tiny woman appeared from the other side of the studio. "We should wear our scars with pride," she declared. "For they contain the history of our suffering and our survival. Is that not right, Aya?"

Aya looked up at her. She could just see her own face in the mirror – blotchy, eyes too bright. She remembered her father saying something similar to a patient who had been disfigured by a roadside bomb, her face badly burned. "Your scars show you are a survivor," he had told her. Aya hadn't understood it then. She still wasn't sure she did now. But she nodded at Miss Helena gratefully, her throat too tight to say anything.

"And these are for you." Miss Helena held in her hands a pair of ballet shoes. Clean pink leather, unworn, elastics carefully sewn in place.

Aya held Miss Helena's eye for a second, then stretched out her scarred leg, seeing the livid white lines reflected in the mirror, telling tales that she would have preferred to keep hidden.

"OK," said Miss Sylvie, as Aya pulled the new shoes on to her feet. "Let us begin."

Aleppo, Syria

There had been a lot of bombs in Aleppo after that first bombardment. By Aya's ninth birthday the rebels and the government were locked in a constant battle, fighting for control of the city. The government used jets and helicopters to strike the rebel-held eastern quarter where Aya and her family lived, while the insurgents shelled the government stronghold in the western half of the city. And then the Russians started bombing them too. At some point Islamic State joined the war; Aya wasn't sure whose side they were on. Sometimes American jets flew over. Dad tried to explain it all to her – whose side everyone was on – but it was too complicated to understand.

Her friend Samia reckoned she could tell the difference between a government bomb and a Russian one just from the sound of the explosion – but Samia said lots of things, especially since her brother Rami had been arrested. She reckoned she was going to be the first female Syrian astronaut in space – and that her hamster contained the spirit of Elvis Presley – and that she was going to mount a covert rescue operation to spring Rami from wherever he was being held. So who knew with Samia!

Mumma was pregnant with Moosa by then. If she hadn't been, they would have left the city sooner. Then Aya wouldn't have been playing out in the street that day and everything would have been different.

Samia was there. And Kimi had brought her little sister, Ifima, who had just started in the baby ballet class at Madam Belova's. The little girl sat on the pavement, playing with a new Barbie doll while the older kids fought over the ball in the dust. It was the usually quiet Kimi who had bet the boys that the girls could beat them at football – only it turned out they were better at pirouettes than penalties!

Aya was about to take a shot on goal when the bombardment happened. Kimi and Samia were shouting encouragement. And then their voices were blown up in a fury of noise.

She remembered being thrown to the ground and feeling rubble raining down like snow. She remembered the sound that felt as if it would burst her eardrums. She remembered the pain.

Then nothing. Suddenly nothing.

When she looked up, the neighbourhood kids looked like pale white ghosts, walking through a fog of dust. She could hear screaming and shouting. And her leg didn't seem to work any more. It was covered in white dust and red blood. She couldn't feel anything.

Then she saw.

Another piece of shrapnel had hit Kimi's little sister, Ifima, and killed her instantly. Her Barbie doll fallen in the dust beside her. Kimi was a white ghost crouched beside her, cradling her – her voice a high-pitched wail of anguish. Samia had her arms wrapped round her and both were pale as clouds.

Miss Helena had said that you should wear your scars with pride. Because they showed you had survived.

But Aya knew they were also a reminder of those who had not.

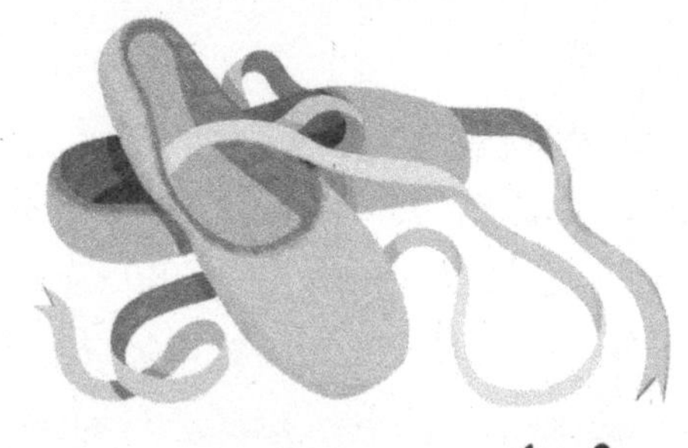

Chapter 14

"So would it be weird to ask what happened to your leg?" asked Dotty.

The other girls had left quickly at the end of the class.

"You were amazing today," said Grace shyly.

"Yeah, well done," added Lilli-Ella with an awkward blush. "Especially, you know with…" She glanced down at Aya's leg.

But then Ciara grabbed Lilli-Ella by the arm and whispered something as they headed off down the stairs, Grace and Blue in tow, and suddenly they were all giggling, leaving Aya standing at the top of the stairs. Ciara glanced back with a smirk and then she and the others were gone.

Dotty and Aya were staying to help with the younger

class, and Dotty had insisted on sharing her packed lunch while they waited.

"I mean, don't tell me what happened if you don't want to," said Dotty, munching on a peanut butter and apple sandwich. "It's none of my business and I'm basically being nosy, so if I'm putting my giant foot in it or saying the wrong thing just tell me to shut up. Everyone else does – I really don't mind."

"There was a bomb," Aya said quietly. "I was playing in the street with my friends and it – it went off."

"Whoa – was anyone ... killed?" Dotty pulled a face. "Or is that weird of me to ask?"

Aya just nodded, thinking of little Ifima, proud as punch in a powder-blue leotard at her first dance lesson. Dotty's expression changed.

"I'm sorry, I shouldn't have asked," said Dotty. "It's just – your life makes mine seem really boring. I mean, school – ballet – school – eat – sleep – homework – more ballet."

Aya didn't look at her. "That sounds … nice."

"Of course, you're completely right." Dotty sighed theatrically. "Compared to what you've been through my life is safe, and all that." But as she said it she sighed again, and bit mournfully into her sandwich.

They both sat in silence for a bit. The tick of the

clock and the humming of the pipes sounded loud and insistent. Dotty shared a packet of raisins and they both sat munching the sweet sticky fruit.

"So – um, where do you go to school?" Dotty asked eventually. "I mean, I know it's summer holidays right now, but when term starts..."

"Nowhere," said Aya.

"Seriously? I thought everyone had to go to school."

"If we are allowed to stay in the UK, maybe then I can find a school," said Aya. "And a nursery for Moosa."

"That's your little brother, right?"

Aya nodded.

"I've always wished I had a sibling," Dotty said with a grin. "Someone to share the crushing weight of parental expectations!"

Aya glanced at her curiously. Dotty was smiling, but her expression had none of its usual sparkle. In an instant she lit up again. "So did Miss Helena give you the whole 'I have always relied on the kindness of strangers thing'?"

As she said it, Dotty adopted a pose uncannily like Miss Helena: chin up, head tilted, beady eyes flashing, with a slight Eastern European twang in her voice. Then she tottered across the floor, her movements exactly mirroring those of the dance teacher, declaiming, "I came to this country with nothing but the shoes on my feet and the desire to dance."

Aya couldn't help smiling as Dotty flopped back into her own self again. "You know, Miss Helena was a great dancer in her time." Dotty nodded up to a framed picture on the wall.

"That's Miss Helena?" Aya stood up to take a closer look at the faded black-and-white print of a dancer in a gorgeous snowy-white tutu. She was holding an arabesque like a bird in flight.

"Oh yeah. You must've heard of Helena Rosenberg? She danced all over the world."

The name was familiar from her ballet books. Aya tipped her head to one side and tried to trace the older woman's expression in the young dancer's face.

"She came to England during the war," Dotty went on. "Not your war. The one that was like a million years ago. With Hitler and everything."

Aya kept staring at the photograph. Miss Helena was an émigré from war – just like her.

"Yeah, she was a Jewish refugee," said Dotty. "At least, I think that's what my mum said."

Dotty sighed heavily again – a sigh Aya couldn't quite figure out. Aya wanted to ask her more – about Miss

Helena, about Dotty's family – but at that moment the first of the little girls came stomping up the stairs and the opportunity was lost.

Maybe Aya wasn't the only one with a story to tell.

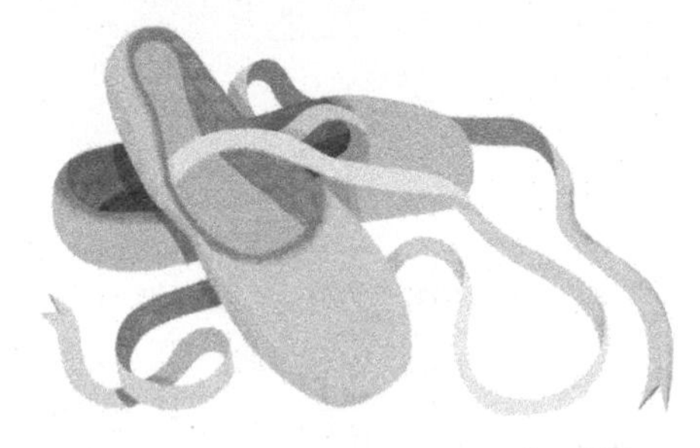

Chapter 15

The rule at the dance school, as Dotty told her, was that parents were to drop off and pick up only. Even the smallest dancers had to put on their own shoes and take care of their own belongings.

"Miss Helena reckons it makes us self-sufficient," Dotty explained. "But I think it's mainly to stop the whole pushy parent 'dance mums' thing. Which totally works for me!"

Dotty grinned before turning to the little ones who were clustering round her – little dancers of five and six, with round tummies and soft limbs in little pink leotards, who gazed at the older girls as if they were prima ballerinas. Aya remembered looking at the big girls like that when she had first started at

Madam Belova's.

She remembered little Ifima looking at her like that once upon a time too.

"Who is your friend, Dotty?" asked a tiny girl with small round blue glasses perched on her freckly nose.

"This is Aya. She's going to be a helper too, Colette!"

"Can she dance as nicely as you, Dotty?"

"Is she as funny as you, Dotty?"

"Oh, she's a loads better dancer than me, Ainka!" Dotty laughed. "Just you wait and see!"

"When are you going to leave us and go to the Royal Northern, Dotty?" This was a little blonde girl with neat French plaits and her knickers sticking out of her leotard.

"I have to get through the final audition first, remember, Margot?

Aya glanced curiously at Dotty, who looked at her and shrugged.

"What's an audition, Dotty?" asked the first girl, her glasses slipping off her nose as she spoke.

"It's like a spelling test or a ballet exam," said Dotty. "Only much more scary!"

"But you told us you wanted to be an actress, Dotty," said Colette with a small frown. "A singing and dancing one!"

"Yes, I did, didn't I!" said Dotty, the shadow flittering across her face again. "And maybe if I don't get in, I still can be. One can but dream!"

Aya looked at Dotty curiously again, but still said nothing.

"Are you going to go too, Aya?" This was the little girl Dotty had addressed as Ainka – small with ebony skin and eyes as bright as two marbles. She had slipped her hand into Aya's and did not let go.

"No… I'm…"

"She should," said Dotty. "She's so good. She does the most beautiful pirouettes I've ever seen."

"Is that the spinny-round one?" asked Margot, eyes bright as she looked at Aya. "I wish I could do that!"

Aya remembered her struggles to acquire the tricky move. Madam Belova telling her to fix her eyes on a spot on the wall, keeping her chin level. "Delay the turn of the head a little," she said. "Then quickly bring it round in advance of your body. That way you won't get dizzy. Nice. Hold your shoulders level and your hips square. That's it! Lovely!" She remembered practising over and over on the roof terrace at home. Fixing her eyes on the minaret of the Maysaloon Mosque as the sun set over the rooftops, feeling the dust under her feet, hearing the sounds of the city – the call to prayer, the traffic far below, the faint tinkle of Mumma's radio. Spinning, spinning.

"I couldn't do it for a long time," she told the little girls.

"And you should see her now!" grinned Dotty. "She's like a Syrian spinning sensation!"

Miss Helena had a very different style with the younger class. Gentler somehow, while still pushing them to be the best they could be.

"Tummy buttons to the front, my little ladies," she said, crouching down to look at their feet as they practised "good toes" and "naughty toes", straightening their arms, gently pushing in their little tummies.

She glanced up at Dotty and touched her very lightly as she went past. "Raise your chin just a tiny bit more, Dotty. See how that makes her look even more like a princess if she lifts her chin, girls?"

Colette had a dreamy expression and her glasses kept slipping off her nose as she danced; Margot looked like a baby meerkat, wobbling in her *développements*, while little Ainka thudded like a baby elephant on flat feet.

But Miss Helena treated them all like prima ballerinas.

"When I was a little girl – a very long, long time ago

in a city far, far away from here – I would spend time in the playground or queuing for the shops just standing on one leg, like a – how is it called – a flamingo!" she told them, adopting a flamingo pose that made the little ones giggle.

"My *maminka* would say, 'What are you doing, little one?' and I would say, 'Nothing, *Maminka*!' but I would keep standing like that, every day. And that is how I get my balance so nice!"

The little ones stared at her, round-eyed, trying to imagine this old lady as a little girl in a land far away. Aya tried to imagine it too. The old lady … the beautiful dancer in the picture … the long-ago little girl who had grown up in a war-torn country just like Aya herself had. Where did Dotty say she had come from?

"Then one day, we were not able to go to school, my sister Elsa and I," said Miss Helena, still holding the *retiré* position, without the slightest wobble.

"Why weren't you able to go to school?" asked Ainka.

"Oh, some bad men said that we could no longer learn with the other children," said Miss Helena with a wave of her hand, as though this was not the important part of the story. "But Elsa and I, we did not mind. We spent all that day – and the next day – and many days after that, learning our lessons at home. But instead of doing it sitting on our bottoms, we would do it standing just on the one leg – so!" She extended her foot gracefully into a *battement fondu*, her arm and her leg arriving in second position together, the whole movement smooth and effortless.

"What happened then, Miss Helena?" said little Colette.

"We got very good at standing on one leg!" said Miss Helena with a smile. "But not so good at mathematics!" She laughed and brought her leg down, and her feet snapped sharply back into fifth.

"Now, let's tuck those little bottoms in, my angels. We want flamingos, not the ugly ducklings. You too, Aya. And your leg can be a weensy and teensy bit straighter. Nice! Look, now she has legs like pencils. This is what we want."

Only little Margot had asked about the scar on Aya's leg, and then only so she could show her the scabs on her own knees. "Where I felled down in the playground. Did you fall down too, Aya?"

Aya just nodded and smiled. "Yes. I fell down too."

She loved the way the little ones saw her as just another dancer. Not a refugee. A nuisance. A victim. Just a big girl in a leotard who could do a pirouette. She wished the older girls could do the same.

"Now I'm going to tell you a story," said Miss Helena, as the little ones gathered round her to learn their new dance. "About a little girl who is carried away on Christmas Eve to the land of the dolls. Do you know that story perhaps?"

Some of the little ones nodded. Others looked wide-eyed with anticipation. Aya smiled. Her father had taken her to see Ahmad Joudeh dance in *The Nutcracker* at the Institute for Dramatic Arts in Damascus as part of the dance festival. It was for her sixth birthday. Before any of the fighting had started. When she had only just started ballet herself. She remembered the long, dark drive home, half sleeping, half dreaming of the dancers on the stage. The headlights dancing on the road. Her father's warm arms carrying her to bed, humming the music. But mostly she remembered the spinning figures on the stage – the way they spun the music into magic, like candyfloss.

"So this is the moment where the little girl – Clara – is carried away to a new land, far away," Miss Helena explained. "Listen carefully and see if you can hear her story. It must have been very frightening to be taken far from her home – so?"

The notes from *The Nutcracker* started to spill across the room and Aya felt the flutter of butterfly wings in her stomach. The music was the same here as it had been that night so long ago. At the theatre, sitting beside Dad, in a new pink dress, watching the story unfold like magic.

Ahmad Joudeh, the wonderful dancer who had played the role of the Nutcracker Prince, had later danced in the ruins of the bombed Palmyra Theatre before fleeing Syria. She had read somewhere that he now danced in Holland. His story had a happy ending of sorts.

"Listen for the story," Miss Helena told the little ones. "You must always try to tell a story as you dance."

"How do we tell stories with no words, Miss Helena?" said Ainka.

"With your fingers, with your toes, with the shapes of your body, with your eyes," said Miss Helena. "The technique, the steps, the precision – all of that is important, but allowing yourself to feel, telling the story with your dance – this is what matters most of all."

Aleppo, Syria

It was after Aya had recovered from the shrapnel wound – when she had started dancing again – that Dad began making plans to leave Syria.

Everyone was talking about leaving by then; so many families had already gone. The city where Aya had lived all her life no longer felt safe. They were being shelled all the time. There were roadside bombs and shootings in the streets, the threat of incursions from Isis forces. Madam Belova's dance studio had been hit and she'd had to move to the basement of the community centre, where they used chairs instead of barres, and where there were no mirrors, sometimes no electricity – just dingy candlelight and a CD player whose batteries ran down, leaving Madam Belova to hum the familiar tunes.

But still Aya did not want to leave.

"After the baby is born and Mumma is well enough, then we will go," Dad told Aya at breakfast one morning after a particularly bad bombing raid.

"But what about my dancing?" All Aya could think about in those days was ballet. The war, the bombs, none of that seemed as important as dancing – and she couldn't bear to leave Madam Belova's. Not when her leg was only just better. She'd already lost so much time.

"There are dancing schools in England!" Dad said, his mouth turned up into a smile but his almond eyes looking tired and anxious. "Other dancing teachers too."

"But they won't be Madam Belova!" Aya had insisted, tears in her eyes.

Dad put his arm round her then. "Habibti," *he said. "Even when you could not go to class because of your leg, even when you were laid up in bed, you were still dancing. I could see it. If you weren't up on your feet you were dancing in your head, making up stories with your fingers and toes. Sometimes I swear I could see your arms going through repetitions in your sleep. That is what it means to be a dancer. The barre, the studio – they are just accessories."*

Aya tried to smile but she still felt anxious as Dad pulled her tight.

"It is no longer safe to stay here. We need to get out while we still can," he said. "But wherever we go to, wherever we end up, you will always dance, habibti. *Because dancing is in your heart, so you carry it with you everywhere."*

"Do you promise, Dad?"

Her father lifted her chin so that she was looking at him and this time his smile reached all the way up to his eyes. "I promise, habibti!"

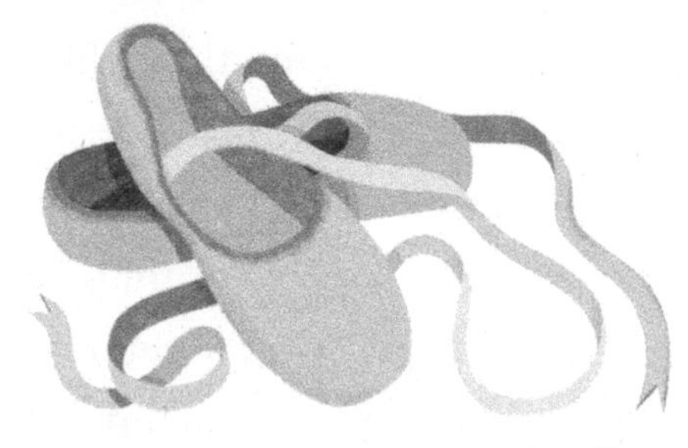

Chapter 16

After the lesson, Aya asked Dotty about what the little ones had said. Both girls were perched on the wall outside the community centre, waiting for Dotty to be picked up. Aya had collected Moosa, who was asleep in his pushchair, his face and hands still sticky from ice cream the food-bank ladies had given him.

"My mum is always late!" Dotty said. "She's never *actually* forgotten me though! Not yet, that is!"

The two girls sat on the low red-brick wall, Dotty scuffing her feet rhythmically along the grey concrete pavement. The day was hot, which Dotty said was pretty unusual for Manchester.

"I think it rains, like, every two days, and twice as

much in leap years – or something like that. I read it somewhere," said Dotty, who wore a leopard-print bomber jacket paired with cartoon-strip leggings and gem-encrusted Converse. Somehow the strange combination suited her. "Don't get too used to the sunshine, that's all I'm saying," she added with a grin.

Aya sometimes wondered if she'd ever get used to anything in Manchester. Even the colours were so different from home. The grey concrete, red bricks, white sky, smatterings of green grass. And England smelled different too. She wondered if every country had its own smell that made locals feel at home and outsiders feel ... alien.

"Is it true you have an audition?" She sounded the unfamiliar word out, glancing down at her own feet in Mumma's old sandals – so drab next to Dotty's sparkly new Converse. "For a ballet school? The Royal Northern?"

Dotty sighed loudly. "Yup – why do you think I spend so much of my life here at the moment? I mean, it's supposed to be the holidays and I'm here every day!"

"That is – very amazing. When is this audition?"

"We already had the prelims," said Dotty with a shrug. "Final auditions are in, like, three weeks."

Aya stared out at the little parade of shops opposite

the community centre, and the high-rise tower blocks rising up beyond them, glass windows glistening in the sunshine. It was hard not to compare it with home. This was a city where dreams had not been blown up in smoke and rubble.

"But you don't really want to go?" said Aya.

"What makes you say that?"

Aya wasn't sure how to explain – how Dotty seemed more alive outside the studio than in it, how her eyes clouded over when she talked about the audition. "Colette said you want to be an actress."

"It's not that I don't like dancing," said Dotty. "I do. Just not always ballet. What I'd really love to do is musical theatre – acting, singing, dancing, the whole lot."

Then she was leaping up, on to the wall, arms thrown wide, toe-tapping and jazz-hands waving with her head back, belting out, "There's no business like show business!" as if she was in the spotlight on Broadway. And then she came to a stop, her shoulders slumped, and she plonked herself back down again. "But, you know, you can't have everything – right?"

"Right," said Aya.

"Ciara is trying out for the Royal Northern," Dotty added, pulling a face. "So we have to go to extra audition sessions with Miss Helena, plus I'm supposed to practise at home – like, all the time! If I'm not eating, sleeping or on the toilet, I'm supposed to be training."

"At home?" Aya glanced at Dotty

"Yeah, we have a studio at home. I have to do two hours every morning." Dotty sighed, looked Aya in the eye, shrugged, then declared, "OK. I suppose I had better tell you."

"Tell me...?"

"I'm sorry I didn't before. I mean, you'll get all the other stuff. It's just I've been putting it off cos people start acting dead weird once they know."

"I don't ... understand?"

"My mother." Dotty stared out at the street where a man in a white van was having an argument with the owner of the kebab shop opposite. "Have you heard of Bronte Buchanan?"

Aya shook her head.

"Well, that's a relief!" Dotty grinned, but she was fiddling with the sleeve of her crazily patterned jacket and she didn't look Aya in the eye. "For a rather small woman, my mother is a very large shadow to grow up under. 'The most famous British dancer since Darcey Bussell' – that's what everyone calls her!"

"Oh," said Aya. "I see."

"Yup! Everyone's always expecting me to be like her. Prima ballerina and all that. Only I'm totally not! And no one has ever stopped to ask if I want to be."

Aya glanced at Dotty. She didn't look up. The smile had faded from her face.

From far off, Aya could hear the sound of a police siren. The men across the road were still arguing. Two kids whizzed past on scooters with lights in the wheels.

"Mum trained with Miss Helena too, you see. She 'spent the happiest years of her life' there – as she is constantly reminding me." Dotty sighed, shrugged and looked up with a wry grin. "So I'm supposed to be having the time of my life too. And I'm trying, but…" She tailed off.

"You are a beautiful dancer also," said Aya, not knowing what else to say.

"Yes, I suppose I am," said Dotty, without a hint of pride or boastfulness. In fact, her tone was, if anything, slightly regretful. "And ballet is the only kind of dancing worth doing, apparently. Why would anyone want to do any other kind of dancing – that's what Mum says! Tap is tacky, modern is undisciplined and as for hip-hop … don't get my mother started on that! If I dared mention that I wanted singing and acting lessons she'd probably have a heart attack.

So vulgar! So that's that, I suppose."

Both girls sat in silence for a moment. The man opposite got into his van, slammed the door and screeched off. The two scooter kids turned in slow circles outside the chip shop.

"Listen to me – going on about my problems," Dotty said, giving herself a shake. "When your home got bombed to bits and you don't even know if you're going to be allowed to stay in England. Moaning about ballet school and a pushy dance mum sounds so lame."

"It doesn't," said Aya, and she meant it.

"What about your mum," said Dotty, with a little shake of the head. "What's she like, anyway?"

Aya thought of her own mumma. Fading away, not glistening like a star.

"She is unwell," she said. One of the kids was doing stunts on his scooter, making it bunny-hop along the pavement, lights flashing. "The journey – it made her sick."

"Sick how? When did it start?"

How could she explain? That Mumma had still been recovering from the birth of Moosa when they left Aleppo. That there hadn't been enough food. That by the time they reached the refugee camp in Turkey she was feverish and dangerously dehydrated. That the winter they had spent there had been freezing, and hundreds had died from the cold. How could Dotty possibly understand all that? It didn't seem fair to even tell her.

"We were in a camp in Turkey."

"A camp?"

"A refugee camp." Aya bit her lip. "It started there. And then after that she get … got worse."

Dotty looked at her curiously for a moment. "We're not so different, are we – you and me," she said.

Aya wanted to ask her what she meant, but at that moment a car drew up on the opposite side of the road. A glossy black four-by-four with tinted windows, one of which rolled down to reveal a glamorous-looking woman. She had large, expressive dark eyes, black hair pulled back into an elegant chignon and a long, slender neck. She wore no make-up but her face seemed to glow in the same way that Dotty's did, though her skin was much lighter than her daughter's.

She had evidently been talking to someone on the phone for she seemed distracted. "Just one second, Marcus. I'm picking up my daughter. Dots! Jump in quick. I'm in a terrible rush."

Dotty was already on her feet. "Mum," she was saying, as she gathered her things hastily together.

"This is Aya – remember, I told you. She's from Syria."

Bronte Buchanan took in Aya for the first time, her gaze distracted. "Yes, Marcus, hold on a sec…" she said to the invisible caller.

Aya was aware of how she must look. Wearing one of Dotty's old leotards and the jogging pants from the clothing bank, a headscarf pulled over her head, and Mumma's tatty sandals slipped hastily on to her feet. With a grubby-looking baby in an old pushchair.

"Hello…" she started to say.

Bronte Buchanan's face was unreadable as she said simply, "Nice to meet you, Aya. Dotty, jump in. We need to go…" Then her attention was back to the invisible Marcus. "Yes, yes, tell them I'll get right on to it. I'm on my way."

Dotty turned to Aya and shrugged before jumping into the car. The tinted window rolled up and the car took off, leaving Aya sitting on the low wall, alone once more.

Chapter 17

Aya arrived back at the bedsit to find Mumma had made food – just beans on toast, cooked on the two-ring stove in the corner, but it was the first meal she had prepared for a long time. She smiled when she saw Aya. A tight, anxious smile, but a smile – that was something.

"You're feeling better?" Aya asked, thinking for some reason of Bronte Buchanan, in her big black four-by-four, with her manicured nails and wrists jangling with bracelets.

"Yes. And I have good news, Aya," said Mumma. She was wrapped in a new cardigan, her hands shaking nervously as she served up the food on to plates.

Aya's stomach lurched. "Is it Dad?"

Mumma shook her head quickly, blinking hard, the tight smile slipping a little.

Aya's heart sank, but she tried to hide her disappointment. "Did you speak to the housing people? Did they sort out the rent?"

Another brief, nervous shake of the head.

"Oh." A pulse of anxiety fluttered in Aya's stomach.

"Your Miss Helena brought this." Mumma held out a brochure and Aya stared at it, confused, still thinking of the landlord's threat to throw them out. The picture on the front was of a young ballerina in practice clothes, standing at the barre with her leg gracefully extended in *arabesque penchée*.

"Royal Northern Ballet School? This is where Dotty is going." Then she thought of her friend's mournful expression and added, "That is – it's where her mum wants her to go."

Mumma sat down then, kneeling on the floor in front of Aya, taking her hands, the food forgotten. Her fingers felt papery and frail between Aya's own. "And you too," she whispered.

Aya sighed. Mumma was obviously confused. She had sauce on her cheek and her eyes were too bright. She must be tired.

"Mumma. You have to audition to get in here. And

it's too late anyway."

Mumma's hands gripped hers more tightly. "If you get in, they can't send you away from England, even if our appeal is rejected. Miss Helena says—"

"When did you speak to Miss Helena?" Aya could feel her mother's fingers clasped round hers. She felt tired and suddenly not hungry.

"She said the audition is in just a few weeks."

Aya stared at the brochure again then glanced at her Mumma's too-bright eyes and wavering smile. "Mumma, I missed the prelim rounds. It's too late."

"This is a chance for you, Aya," said Mumma, her voice more urgent now, her fingers still gripping Aya's. "Even if Moosa and I have to leave."

Aya felt her stomach contract. "I told you – I won't let that happen."

Mumma pulled her hand away and placed the brochure in Aya's grip. "This is what your dad would have wanted," she said quietly.

Mumma hadn't said Dad's name for so long. Hearing it now sent a shock, like electricity, through Aya. And the expression in Mumma's eyes as she said it frightened her somehow.

"Sure, Mumma," she said, leading her over to the bed, sitting her down gently. Mumma was obviously confused, but Aya didn't want to upset her any more. "Sure, OK. I'll talk to Miss Helena tomorrow. OK?"

"Promise?" said Mumma.

"Yes, Mumma. I promise. Now, sit still and I will finish the supper."

Aleppo, Syria

Dad always planned things carefully. Once he had decided that they had to leave, he dug out Aya's school atlas. He couldn't print off more detailed maps because there was no power, and anyway, it was too risky, he said, to have such things in the house. He even hid the atlas under the mattress, but took it out every night to pore over as Mumma slept on the sofa, arms wrapped protectively round her ballooning belly. Aya would crouch on the floor next to him as Dad traced his long fingers across the contours of the maps in the atlas – along the rivers, following highways, over mountains and lakes … talking her through the long journey they would make: Turkey, Greece, then onwards … all the way to England.

Once the baby was born then they would go – to safety, he said. It was too dangerous to leave while Mumma was pregnant. And the baby was due in just a few weeks now. It wouldn't be long…

But then – just before Mumma's due date – government forces surrounded the rebel-held area of the city, cutting off the escape route along the road that led north to Turkey. There was no way out of the city in either direction. They were stuck. No supplies coming in. No way out.

Now Aya understood the meaning of the word 'siege.'

Moosa was born at home during an airstrike. There were complications with the birth, Dad said. Aya didn't really understand. She only knew that Mumma lost a lot of blood. She would need time to recover.

Aya looked after her new brother a lot in the early days because Mumma was so unwell and Dad was needed at the hospital all the time – coping with the casualties of the war who kept pouring in, working with fewer and fewer resources because the city was cut off from outside supplies – sometimes without electricity.

Aya remembered sitting in the dark apartment in a blackout, singing to baby Moosa by candlelight. Maybe that was why she felt like a second mother to him sometimes.

She had never understood until then what it meant to be hungry. But government troops had cut supply routes to the city and after weeks of food shortages, there were stories of people eating grass and leaves. Luckily Dad had stock-piled provisions, but still they had to be careful. Mumma no longer baked manoushi *bread or* mahashi *and there were no almonds or fruit in the market, where the stalls were all bare. Nobody knew how long the siege would last.*

"Why is our own government attacking us?" Aya asked Dad.

Dad sat in the kitchen with Moosa asleep in his arms. Moosie was so tiny then – small and red-faced, with a shock of dark hair and long eyelashes.

"The world has turned upside down, habibti,*" Dad said. "Let us hope it turns the right way back again soon!"*

"Will we stay here now? Forever?"

Dad's face creased into a frown. His almond eyes looked full of something Aya did not understand. "No, Aya. We have to leave. I don't know how just yet, but somehow we have to get out of Syria."

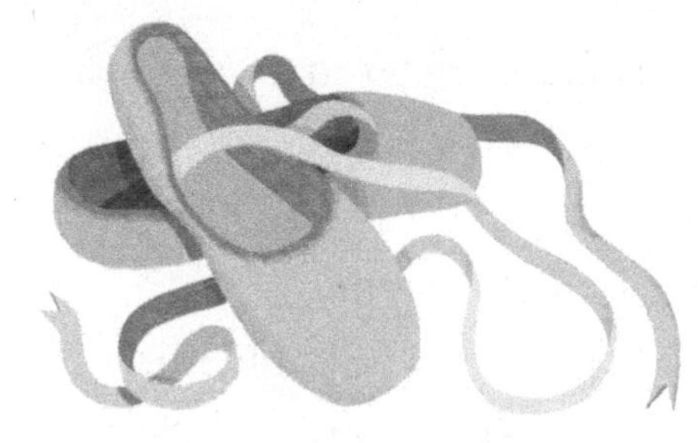

Chapter 18

"I used to dance when I was younger," said Mrs Massoud, her lined and anxious face lit up with one of her rare, twinkling smiles. She had offered to take Moosa to the park while Aya went to ballet upstairs. "And so did my Milena – ballroom and Latin. There was a beautiful ballroom in Damascus; it's gone now."

Her eyes were bright as she talked and Aya thought of her crying every night. Of the picture of her daughter she always kept in her wallet. Of her bag of papers about her lost son.

The people left behind.

"Are you sure – about Moosa?" said Aya.

"Don't you worry about a thing," said Mrs Massoud,

taking Moosa out of Aya's arms and planting a kiss on his warm cheek. "I see all you do, for your mother and the little one. You go. Enjoy your dancing! I shall be happy having a little one to spoil!"

Aya gave Moosa a kiss and told him to be a good boy. "Don't you be a pickle for Mrs Massoud, Moosie!" she said. "And keep an eye on Mumma for me, OK?"

The relief she felt as she raced upstairs tore at her insides. She had promised to look after her baby brother, but sometimes she couldn't wait to get away from him.

She wanted to talk to one of the teachers before class began, but Miss Sylvie was on the phone in the office and there was no sign of Miss Helena. Aya started to put on her ballet shoes, thinking she could warm up before the others arrived.

"Yes, Bronte, I understand, but there's nothing to worry about," Miss Sylvie's voice was clearly audible through the doors. "I understand that Dotty needs to focus… No, Aya will not be a distraction…"

With a jolt of shock, Aya realised they were talking about her.

"Bronte, come on! Dotty is doing well. Yes, she sometimes lacks focus but she's been working a lot harder recently. There's no reason to think that Aya will be a problem."

Aya felt her cheeks burn and her stomach turned painfully. That was how Dotty's mother saw her. A poor little refugee girl. A problem. Now she understood the look in the woman's eyes the day before.

"Actually, I think it will be good for Dotty," Miss Sylvie was saying. "And Aya deserves this chance..."

But Aya didn't want to hear any more. She made her way quickly into the studio and started working on limbering exercises, trying to drown out the words that kept turning round in her head: "... a distraction ... a problem..."

When the other girls arrived for class, she tried not to let any of them see how close she was to tears. Dotty was late as usual, and she had the feeling that the others had been talking about her as they all fell silent when they came in and saw her at the barre.

"Here's our refugee dancer!" said Ciara.

"Don't call her that, Ciara," said Lilli-Ella, glancing nervously at Aya.

"Yeah, it's really not nice," said Grace, but she coloured as she spoke.

"If you say so," said Ciara. But the word was already out there, weaving its way through the air, creating an invisible barrier that ran between Aya and the others, even after Dotty bounced into the room, grinning, laughing, giving her a giant hug.

But Aya decided that she would not let them see how much it hurt her. Instead, she threw all she was feeling into her dancing, letting a little of the locked-up emotions trickle out through her feet, through her hands. Not too much – if she let out all she was feeling she felt as if she might break, fall into pieces, shatter – but just a little felt like a relief.

At the end of the class, Miss Helena kept her back. "Are you OK, Aya?" she asked. "You don't look happy today."

"No – I am... I—" But the words stuck in her throat and made her cheeks burn.

"Did your *maminka* talk to you about the Royal Northern?"

"Yes, but I think she was ... confused, maybe?" said Aya.

"No confusion," said Miss Helena. "I think you stand a chance. If it is something you want."

Aya's heart leapt, but the thought of Bronte Buchanan's words was still racing round her head.

"We won't have long to get you ready," Miss Helena was saying.

"But Dotty said... I mean, I have missed the prelims."

"Yes – this is true. I will have to make a few phone calls," said Miss Helena. "But in such circumstances, an exception can perhaps be made."

Aya's heart soared – just for a second – then fell.

"But the appeal..." Aya managed to say. "And the landlord. What if ... we don't know if we are allowed to stay."

"We will cross that bridge if we come to it," said Miss Helena with a wave of her hand.

Dad always used to say that. About crossing bridges when you came to them. Not worrying about stuff that might never happen. But Dad wasn't around any more and Aya had learned to be more wary – less trusting – since he had gone.

"You have been through a lot, *kochana*," said Miss Helena with a curious tilt of her head. "Maybe it is time to let some good things happen to you."

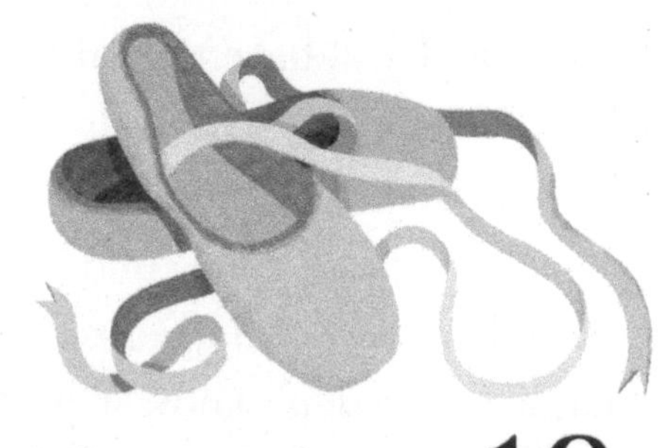

Chapter 19

"Anyone can apply for the Royal Northern," said Miss Sylvie at the beginning of the audition prep class the next day. "Even if they have never had a dancing lesson in their lives."

"Even if they're not English?" Ciara glanced pointedly at Aya.

"The Royal Northern takes pupils from all over the world," said Miss Helena. "And they do not care whether you have passed any ballet exams or danced solo parts. They are looking for an inborn, deep talent for dancing, for musicality, artistry."

Dotty glanced at Aya, rolled her eyes and mouthed, "I am *so* glad you are here!"

"Of course, they are looking for a certain body type

too," said Miss Helena. "Mobile arched feet, flexible joints, a beautifully held head … natural turn-out at the hips is a vital requirement for ballet. All these things will have helped you get through the preliminary rounds."

Aya glanced down at her reflection in the mirror. In Dotty's old leotard, with her hair pulled back off her face, did she look like a dancer?

"But at the final auditions they will be looking for children who truly love ballet –" Miss Helena glanced just for a second at Dotty as she said this. "– Who are willing to work – almost to slave – for the seven years of training. Who are there because it is the only thing in the world they want to do."

Dotty pulled another funny face like she was choking to death. Aya smiled. The thought of dancing for seven years made her feel like she did when she thought of home. But Dotty wanted to sing – to act, to do tap and modern and hip-hop…

"The desire to dance must come from deep down inside the person who is actually going to have to work at it," Miss Helena went on, looking at Dotty again as she spoke. "Not from anyone else – parents, teachers – it must come from you. This is what makes a ballerina truly great."

"But your parents also have to be able to afford the fees, right?" said Ciara.

"Wrong. There are scholarships," said Miss Sylvie, who had come in with some paperwork that the girls needed to sign for the school audition application. "If a student is good enough, the Royal Northern will try to support them financially."

"Even if they are a refugee?" Ciara said the word with such vehemence that Aya felt it like a slap in the face.

"You realise, young lady, that I am a refugee," said Miss Helena, quietly, surveying Ciara with an unreadable expression on her face.

"But—"

"Ah, you think it does not count perhaps – because I came here so many years ago," Miss Helena went on. "Probably around the time of the Romans and the dinosaurs, yes?"

Dotty smirked but Ciara had fallen silent.

"I came to this country seeking refuge from a war that destroyed my home and wanted to destroy my family," said Miss Helena. "Britain opened its arms to me and thousands of others like me."

"I know that, but—" Ciara started to say.

"I am proud to call myself a refugee," Miss Helena

went on. "And Aya should be also. This country is proud to have opened its doors to the poor, the sick and the needy. The only shame is for those who now would close their hearts to those who need protection."

Ciara opened her mouth then closed it again.

"Then we will hear no more talk of this. Let's dance!"

"That shut her up!" Dotty whispered to Aya as they made their way to the barre. But Aya glanced at Ciara and saw her tightly pursed lips and the sharp glimmer of her eyes as she started to limber up. And she was not so sure.

The class was incredibly hard work. Miss Helena demanded absolute perfection, so every muscle, every move and line was under scrutiny. And the other two were more advanced than she was, so Aya spent a lot of time playing catch-up. But she still felt a thrilling tick of excitement; her body seemed to hum with the sheer joy of dancing again.

At the end of the class Miss Helena talked to them about their audition dances.

"Each girl has the chance to perform a solo," she explained. The girls sat on the floor, Dotty attempting to retie her frayed ribbons, Ciara glancing at her own reflection in the long mirrors. It was starting to get dark outside, and the pink, late sunshine cast odd shadows across the linoleum in a way that reminded Aya of Madam Belova's studio.

"The dance has to reflect who you are. Where you have come from, and where you want to go – your memories, your hopes, your dreams," Miss Helena went on. "So next time we meet I want you to bring a few objects that mean something to you."

"What sort of objects?" asked Dotty.

"This is up to you," said Miss Helena. "Treasured possessions, photographs. Things that show who you are. That tell your story."

So many of the objects Aya cared about were long-lost – back in Syria, under rubble by now, perhaps. Lost forever in a world that was gone.

"I don't see what that's got to do with our audition dance," said Ciara.

"It has everything to do with the way you choreograph your piece," said Miss Helena.

"*We* choreograph them?" said Ciara.

Miss Helena just smiled. "Exactly. Bring your objects to the next class. And we will weave stories, OK?"

Chapter 20

But Aya couldn't make it to class the next day, or the day after that. The landlord had agreed to let them stay till the end of the month but time was running out and there was still no sign of the paperwork. And Mumma's headache did not go away. It got so bad that if she tried to get out of bed, she felt dizzy and sick. She wouldn't go and see a doctor, so Sally at the centre gave Aya some over-the-counter pain pills for Mumma, but they didn't seem to make it any better.

More days passed. Aya didn't like to leave Mumma alone for too long. When Moosa got restless she took him down to the park, where she pushed him on the swings and spun him as fast as she could on the roundabout, practising her barre exercises by the railings while he played in the sandpit – and wondering whether it was possible to miss something so desperately that it could make you ill. Maybe that was really what had made Mumma unwell too. Homesickness.

After a week, Mumma was thinner and more tired than Aya had ever seen her. She had barely eaten all week. She wasn't even crying any more – as if the well of her sadness had dried her out inside.

"I am sorry," she said to Aya, over and over again. "I am so sorry, so sorry."

"It's OK, Mumma. I don't mind looking after you," Aya said each time, even though she did mind – sometimes she minded desperately. Dad had told her to look after Mumma and Moosa. And she almost hated him for it. Then hated herself for feeling that way. She pushed away the thought and said again, "I don't mind, Mumma. Really."

"I know it, *habibti*!" said Mumma, using the name Dad had always called her. As if she knew. "But I want you to have your opportunity. To have a life here."

"I will, Mumma," said Aya. "Don't worry about me. You just need to rest now – and get better. Then everything will be fine."

Leaving Aleppo

In the end they left in a hurry. The government and the Russians declared a ceasefire and there were radio announcements urging rebels to surrender and civilians to quit east Aleppo.

Mumma wasn't well enough to move – not really. But Dad said that it was too dangerous to stay. If the government forces took the city there would be reprisals for those who remained. And this might be their only chance. Aya remembered leaving at dawn, hastily grabbing a few last possessions, stuffing her beloved pointe shoes, carefully wrapped, deep into the belly of her bag, joining the river of people making their way to the border. To safety – or so they hoped. Leaving home behind them forever.

So many things they had to leave behind.

Sometimes it felt as if she had left part of herself behind with them.

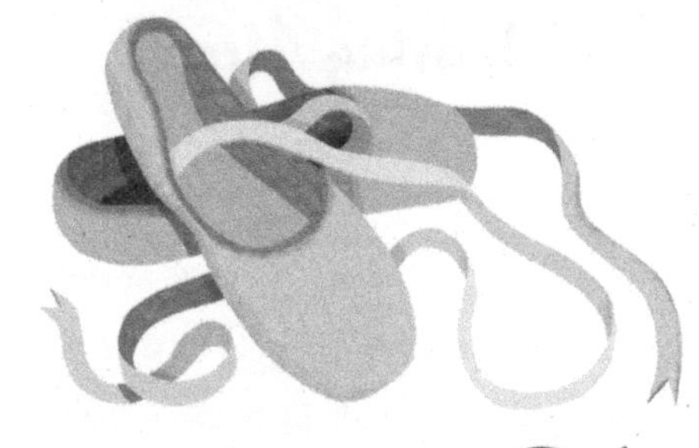

Chapter 21

That night Aya sat in the bedsit, staring at her few meagre possessions. It had been over a week since she had been to Miss Helena's dance studio. Mumma was asleep in the chair. It had not been a good day. She had persuaded Mumma to get out of bed and go to the centre for a bit, while Aya took Moosa to the park. They were only gone for perhaps half an hour, but when they got back Mumma was upset. The landlord had been into the centre, shouting and making more threats. Mrs Massoud said Mumma had dropped a cup of tea, which had smashed, sending hot liquid all over the floor. Even though Sally had cleaned it up and told her it was nothing to worry about, nobody had been able to calm Mumma down after that. Aya had managed to get her home and made her have a shower, but she hadn't been able to persuade her to eat, and Mumma had cried herself to sleep.

Moosa seemed happy though. Aya had tired him out at the park, pushing him on the swings and racing him around the climbing frame, pretending to be monsters, and now he was lying on the rug, thumb in his mouth, staring at the dancing images on a second-hand portable DVD player that Sally said had once belonged to her little nephew.

"Do you remember home, Moosie?" Aya murmured, as Moosa giggled at the antics of a dancing pig on the screen. "Do you remember any of it?"

She glanced again at the contents of her rucksack, which she had laid out on the bed. The bareness of the room and the sparsity of her possessions seemed more glaring than ever as she ran her eyes over the scraps and fragments that were all she had left of her old life. A few bits of clothing, a couple of pictures, a toothbrush.

If she ever made it back to the ballet class, Miss Helena had said to bring items that showed where she had come from. Did that just mean Aleppo? Or was it the refugee camps, the detention centre, the places where they had slept on the beach, and by the road, where they had crossed the border at night, crossed cities and countries on buses and boats, the endless days trapped in the dark of the container, the beach, that night on the sea... Did it mean all those places too?

"Aya, Aya! Up!"

Moosa teetered towards her on his little unsteady feet, clamouring to get up on the bed. Aya swept him up in her arms and he giggled, grabbing her nose and tangling his tiny fists in her hair. She laughed and held him close, smelling his warm baby smell.

"Wherever we go, you always smell the same, Moosie!" she told him in a whisper. Sometimes she wanted to bury her nose in that smell to make the world stand still, make time stop spinning.

She blew a raspberry on his tummy that made him giggle. Then he was reaching out towards the objects on the bed. "Dada, Dada!" he said.

"What is it you want, little man?"

She let him clamber down and he reached immediately for the large spotted handkerchief.

Dad always had a handkerchief on him – large and bright and usually spotted. He had lent this one to Aya when they had caught a lift on the back of a lorry from the Turkish border to the refugee camp at Kilis. Dust had been flying everywhere, making her cough, and Dad had given her the handkerchief and told her to tie it round her mouth. "You look like a bandito!" he had said.

Moosa reached for it now. "Dada," he said again.

"You remember Dada, do you?" said Aya.

She picked up the handkerchief. Sometimes she worried that her own memories of Dad were fading. She could picture his face only in fragments – his eyes, his smile, the small scar on his chin – not all together.

Moosa had grabbed one of the ballet shoes and was trying to put it in his mouth and Aya found herself laughing. "Not for you, monster teeth! But good choice! Those can be for my hopes and my dreams, I suppose."

That was two objects, but Miss Helena had told them to bring four or five. What else did she have to show who she was, where she came from?

She picked up what looked like a small lump of rock and weighed it in her hand. This was all she had left of the street where she had grown up. A piece of rubble she had shoved in her pocket on the morning they had left – belongings hastily shoved in their packs, running for the hills, looking back on the bombed-out buildings that had once been home.

Then she let her fingers trail over a large shell –

brittle, swirled, smashed in one place. This was from the beach in Turkey. Dad had given it to her the day before…

Moosa grabbed for the shell and she held him tight in her arms and squeezed him so he squealed.

She put the shell aside. "Maybe you can be one of my things!" she muttered, pulling one of the tiny socks from Moosa's podgy little feet and kissing his toes. "After all, I don't make much sense without you!"

But Moosa wasn't listening. He had wriggled himself free and was sliding off the bed, pointing at the DVD player. "Piggy!" he said in English.

"Sure," she said. "Let's watch Piggy. Who knows if I'll ever get back to Miss Helena's class anyway."

So she packed away her things and then they lay together on the bed, Moosa curled up in her arms, watching Peppa Pig, dressed as a ballerina, dance in bold flashes of colour across the screen. Eventually they both fell asleep, and Aya dreamed of dancing pigs and Dad's giant handkerchiefs and broken shells and ballet shoes, and all the scattered jigsaw puzzle pieces of who she was dropped along the journey.

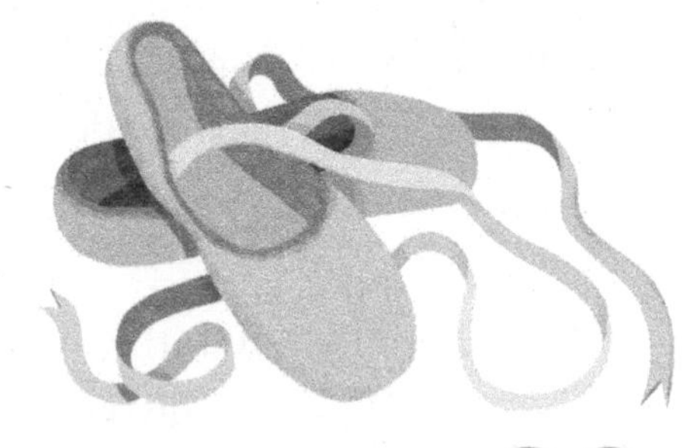

Chapter 22

It was Mrs Massoud who got Mumma out of bed. She came round one afternoon while Aya was getting food and spoke to Mumma for a long time. Aya did not know what they spoke about, but when she returned, Mumma said, "You must not miss any more dance lessons, *habibti.*"

"But you're not well," protested Aya. "And I don't mind—"

"But I do," said Mumma, trying very hard to smile, though it did not reach her eyes. "And I can manage. Mrs Massoud will help."

"But Moosa? And your headaches?"

"I will be OK."

Aya looked at her nervously. Mumma did not seem

any better, but she did seem changed. Whatever Mrs Massoud had said to her had made a difference, because she was adamant that Aya must go back to her dancing.

So the next day Aya returned to the audition class.

"I'm so glad you are back!" said Dotty. "We were worried about you. I thought they'd maybe sent you home. I kept asking at the centre – everyone misses you there. I made friends with your Mr Abdul, by the way. He is so funny! I'm teaching him naughty English words and he is teaching me to tap dance. Did you know he could tap dance?"

"Um – no."

"Well, he's pretty awesome. And Mrs Massoud knows how to tango – and do the American Smooth. Mr and Mrs Massoud are the nicest people, like, ever. I wish they were my grandparents."

"Mumma was sick," Aya said.

"I know. Mrs Massoud was telling me. She's had no news about her son, by the way. Oh, and the food-bank ladies said they miss Moosa! It's been too quiet without him, they said! Although they did say that I cause more trouble than he does!"

Aya smiled at the thought of Dotty hanging out at the centre, befriending the Massouds and playing chess with Mr Abdul – but she wasn't sure Bronte Buchanan would approve. Wouldn't it be a distraction? Shouldn't Dotty be practising?

"And we've started a singing group," Dotty went on. "It was sort of my idea – and the food-bank ladies are in a choir at church so they've been helping. So people come along with songs from the country they came from and we all try and learn them. It's fun, though I have no idea what we're singing about half the time!"

"That sounds nice," said Aya. She thought of the songs she had heard along the way – floating through the camp at Kilis, in the hostel at night, Dad singing to her when the bombs fell. Songs of home, and happiness and heartache. Songs that helped ease the weight of feelings somehow, as dancing did for her.

"But now you're back it's going to be way more fun!" said Dotty, dragging her into class. "Ballet has been super, super boring without you. And there is, like, no time left to get you ready for this audition, you know!"

After warm-up, Aya showed Miss Helena the objects she had brought. The elderly lady looked them over, then nodded thoughtfully. Dotty also had her bag of what she referred to as "bits and bobs", including a fluffy unicorn, a pair of red sparkly shoes, a cushion in the shape of a poo emoji and a picture of her mum dancing in *Swan Lake* at Covent Garden.

"She said they were supposed to reflect who we are!" said Dotty with a grin and a shrug.

Ciara hadn't bought anything. "My father is going to hire a choreographer," she announced. "A professional. To devise a proper dance for me."

"If you wish." Miss Helena did not look surprised. "Then today you will help Aya."

"But this is supposed to be our class – me and Dotty!" Ciara protested. "Our parents are paying. And she didn't even do the prelims!"

"In dance we can always learn from one another," Miss Helena said, waving her hand to dismiss Ciara's objections. "By watching another's process, hearing the stories others have to tell and seeing how they tell them. Aya, let us begin."

Miss Helena's way of working was different from anything Aya had done before. She had brought different pieces of music for them to listen to. She asked Aya to lay her objects out across the studio floor, then sit down in the middle and look at them as she played each piece of music.

"If you want to move, then move," was all she said.

Aya glanced nervously at Dotty, who was sitting by

the door. Ciara sat by the barre, tapping her foot crossly.

"But what should I … do?"

"The time I saw you dancing in the yard, the movements came from within – am I right?"

"Yes, but…"

Aya recalled how unhappy she had felt then. How angry. How she had felt that the dance might break her into small pieces. She didn't feel like that now. She just felt really self-conscious and awkward.

"So listen to the music, think about your objects – and let the dance come from within."

Aya tried. But she couldn't seem to connect the music with the things across the room. She just felt tired, and confused … and stupid.

"I can't…" she said after a few minutes.

Miss Helena sat down next to her. Somctimes Aya could not believe how easily this little old lady moved. She picked up the lump of rock. "From your home?" she asked.

Aya nodded. She felt close to tears. She didn't know what Miss Helena wanted her to do. And Ciara's words were echoing in her ears. "We are paying for this class … she didn't even get through prelims…"

Miss Helena turned it over in her hands. "Your home was bombed?"

"Not my building – but others on our street," Aya said quietly.

"And that is why you had to leave?"

Aya nodded.

"I left my home when I was younger than you are now," Miss Helena said, turning the piece of rock over in her hand. "After the Germans invaded Prague. I left my parents and my whole family."

Aya looked at her in surprise. "You came alone?"

"Many years ago now," she said in a quiet voice. "And this is your father's?" Miss Helena picked up the handkerchief.

Aya managed another brief nod.

"I missed my parents a very great deal when I came to England," said Miss Helena. "You miss your father too, I think."

Aya was silent. It felt wrong to talk of him here. Like she had been cut open and someone was reaching in and touching her beating heart.

Miss Helena seemed to understand this. "It is difficult – even painful – but sometimes we must try to dance from the places that lie closest to our hearts." She replaced the handkerchief with care.

"But – how…?"

"Listen to the music and let it help you feel ... feel

even the most difficult things."

The notes started up again – a new piece that Aya didn't recognise, but which reminded her in an odd way of the call to prayer. Summer evenings on the rooftops. She wrapped her arms round her legs and tried to focus on the ballet shoes, Moosa's sock...

She still didn't know what she was supposed to be doing but she had to do something. She arranged her arms into the gesture for baby, then adopted the classical mime for sleep. She tried to move like Moosa did, unsteady on his feet, toddling then falling. She lifted him up and held him close to her. For a second the music caught her and she thought of kissing his fat little feet, holding him during the blackout when Dad was at the hospital. She could almost smell him in her arms... just for a second – then the self-conscious feeling returned. What now?

She saw the piece of rock and wracked her brains for memories of home. The elegant sitting room that Mumma always kept so smart, the warm smells of *manoushi* bread in the kitchen, the roof terrace where she had seen the first bombs falling on her birthday. She felt herself turn, her body moving involuntarily into the dance she had done for Dad. "Dance for us, *habibti*..."

She stopped in front of Dad's handkerchief on the floor. She wanted to remember his giant sneezes, the smell of him, his almond eyes laughing … but for some reason all she could think of was the dust in the back of the lorry, arriving at the camp, the rows of containers…

And then she looked at the shell and other thoughts started to leak out of the places where she had tightly packed them away. Thoughts of the beach, the boat, in the water…

"I'm sorry, I – I cannot…"

Miss Helena turned the music off. "A good start," she said.

Aya's head was light and her breath came heavily.

"I think we've done enough for tonight," she could hear Miss Helena saying. But Aya felt far away, as though she was at the bottom of an ocean, the memories swilling around her, keeping her under.

"I will leave you girls to warm down. And perhaps, Dotty, you can show Aya your dance?"

Aya turned to her friend, who was still sitting by the door. She looked far away too.

"What about me?" said Ciara.

"You can decide whether you feel there is anything here for you to learn," said Miss Helena.

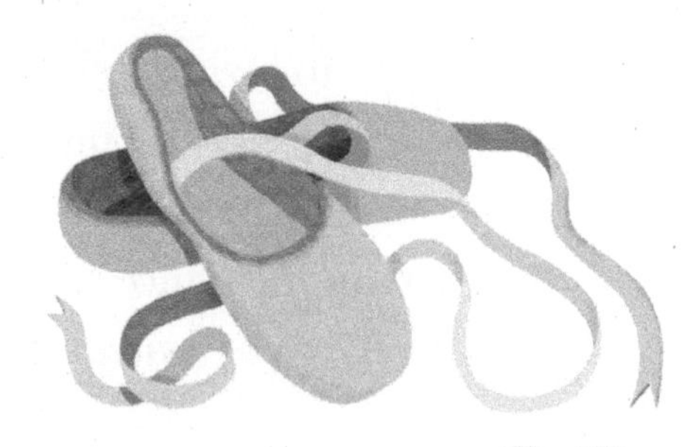

Chapter 23

"Do you want to see it?"

Aya was sitting cross-legged in the corner of the room. Ciara had gone out to get changed, saying she didn't need lessons from Dotty Buchanan, and so it was just the two of them left in the darkening studio.

"Yes! That is, if you don't mind."

"I worked on it while you were away," said Dotty. "I hated doing it at first but then I kind of got into it. I decided to see it as a sort of acting, rather than dancing," she said. "And it doesn't have to be pure ballet so I could be a bit more free – include some of the stuff Mr Abdul showed me. And Mrs Massoud's ballroom stuff too." Then she grinned shyly. "Actually, do you mind if I turn the lights out? It kind of helps."

"Of course." Aya went to switch off the light and the studio fell into a blue and grey gloom. She still felt weirdly disconnected – half her mind still in the sea of memories, the other here in the dance studio.

"It's a bit weird!" Dotty was saying. "Don't judge, OK!"

Dotty pressed play on the CD then ran to position herself in the middle of the floor as the first notes of the piece came on.

The opening of the piece was light-hearted, and Aya saw the clowning Dotty she knew well – leaps and spins designed to entertain; a flicker of a tap dance; old-fashioned somehow – then a moment when she lurched into vibrant hip-hop. And then came a crashing change in tempo and Dotty turned as if there was someone else in the room. Someone whom she wished to please very much. Dotty danced around the invisible person as if this were a ballroom, reaching out, as if pleading to be noticed – a few waltz steps; a tango; an angry paso doble. She was bright-eyed, first loving, then pleading, then angry and defiant.

Aya watched every move; her friend was a truly beautiful dancer. But – more than that – she was a wonderful actress. Aya found it impossible to take her eyes from her.

And then – just for a second – Dotty lit up and became a ballerina, a sugar plum fairy, graceful, light. On the tips of her toes, dancing through a playful *pas de chat* and then into a beautiful *ballonné*.

And then it was over and Dotty wilted, reached out for something that was gone – a few tango steps, an angry flicker of paso doble – then dropped and sparkled into the pretence of happiness for one final pirouette, before the piece came to an end.

She thought of Dotty's objects – the crazy unicorn, the emoji cushion, the red slippers, the picture of her mother. Dotty had told the story so well that Aya could see how each twisted through the dance, how each different style had been blended together to create a beautiful piece of story-telling by a girl who had the heart and soul of an actress.

"What do you think?"

Dotty was on her feet now, glancing at her nervously, breathless and bright-eyed.

"It is … wonderful!" said Aya. "You tell the story so beautifully."

"Yeah, well, Mum says I'm a born show-off! Sometimes I think—" She stopped and shrugged. "Never mind."

It was getting late. The light was dying outside the

windows and the community centre was quiet.

"What?" asked Aya. "What do you think?"

"Oh, it's just I sometimes wonder if I actually told her that I'd rather be doing musical theatre – aiming for the West End rather than Covent Garden – maybe she'd understand. She followed her dream; perhaps she'd understand that this is mine."

"Maybe you should tell her," said Aya.

"Maybe." Dotty sighed then grinned. "But you like the dance – that's the main thing."

Aya wanted to ask her more but she wasn't quite sure how. Sometimes she felt like she'd known Dotty forever and sometimes she realised she hardly knew her at all.

Dotty glanced at her watch. It was later than either of them had realised. The community centre suddenly seemed eerily quiet. Aya could hear the water glugging through the pipes, the low buzz of the electric lights.

"We should probably go," said Dotty, jumping to her feet. "My mum will be here any minute!"

But when she went to the door it wouldn't open. She rattled the handle. "Oh no!"

"What's the matter?"

"I think we're locked in."

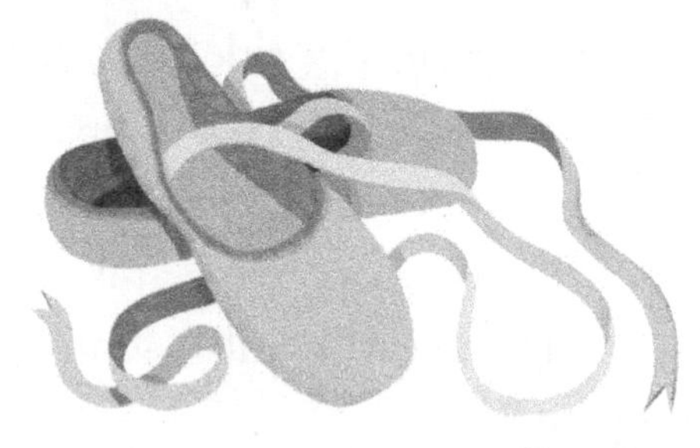

Chapter 24

Aya felt a surge of panic. The studio was a small room with only the skylight for a window. Suddenly it seemed stiflingly close.

She grabbed the door and rattled it, terror rising.

"Don't stress. I'll call Miss Sylvie – oh!" Dotty lifted her hands in dismay. "My phone is in my ballet bag – outside!"

Aya could feel terror beating in her chest. Her lungs felt tight, her head pounding, memories pouring in, clouding her. She slammed her hands against the door.

"Aya, are you OK?"

Dotty had grabbed her by the shoulder. But Aya couldn't focus on her face. Couldn't breathe. Her eyes tore around the room desperately. She could see her own reflection on every side. But memories were pushing in on her, making it hard to breathe.

"I don't like – I don't like … closed spaces," she said.

"Sit down," Dotty was saying, taking her by the shoulder. "Miss Helena will realise soon enough. We'll be out in no time."

But the panic felt like drowning as Dotty led her to the corner, sat her down with her back to the mirror, wrapping a concerned arm round her.

"If nobody comes in ten minutes then we'll smash the glass in, I promise!" She said it jokingly but Aya was shivering now. She felt sick and dizzy.

"You want to tell me about it?" said Dotty.

Aya shook her head.

"I can tell you what I'm most afraid of, if you like," said Dotty. Her arm was round Aya and her voice was gentle. "Mostly I'm scared of letting my mum down. I guess that's what my dance is about, really."

In her head, far away as if at a great distance, Aya could recall Dotty dancing, her arms reaching out to someone – her mum?

"Probably a silly thing to be afraid of, but I just know how much she wants me to be a ballerina – to follow in her footsteps … only sometimes the idea of spending seven years at ballet school makes me feel like I can't breathe."

There was a quietness in Dotty's voice that lay still in the air between them. Aya closed her eyes and tried to breathe in and out, tried to focus on the glugging sound of water in the pipes, the humming of electric lights. After what felt like forever, she started to speak.

"On the journey here," she heard herself saying, her own words sounding distant. "We are smuggling … in a container."

"Like – on the back of a lorry?"

Aya nodded. "There were many, many of us in there. More than thirty. It was the only way to get out of Syria. Because of the fighting – and the border guards…"

"How long?" asked Dotty. Aya could see the two of them reflected in the mirror opposite. Dotty's arm round her, holding her tight. Both faces pale as ghosts in the gloaming, like the faces of the other people in the container.

"Three days, I think."

Aya remembered the dark inside the metal prison. No food, no water, barely enough air to breathe.

"What about… I mean, what if you needed the toilet?"

Aya's eyes were still tightly closed. She could feel Dotty's arm round her, could hear her breathing, and she tried to focus on those feelings.

"They stopped sometimes and let us out, but not always. If there were border guards with guns we had to stay hidden."

"Wasn't it ... dangerous?"

Aya said nothing for a moment. "There was an old lady. A grandma," she started to say.

The Container

Aya remembered the old lady's face – wrinkled like an almond, eyes watery blue, staring at her across the darkness inside the container.

Aya sat with Moosa in her arms, cradling him tight in the darkness, hushing him when he cried. "Crying takes up more air, Moosie," she whispered, although she felt like screaming out loud herself. Screaming and sobbing to be let out. Instead, she tried to slow her breathing, push away the panic that closed in on her in the dark. The darkness that stretched to fill hours and days, filled with sobs, fitful sleep and oxygen-deprived dreams. Aya had heard stories of people smugglers who sold refugees into slavery – of people dying in the back of containers... Those images danced through her dreams.

And then the sound of dogs barking. The door slamming open. White light and cold salty air rushing in. Voices yelling, "Over here! Quick, we need a medic. There must be two dozen people in here."

Blinking in the light. No longer fully aware where she was, or how they had got there. A smell – worse than she'd ever smelled before. Then policemen were clambering inside, carrying people out. When an officer tried to take Moosa out of her arms she clung on tight and would not let them take him.

"Nobody's going to hurt you or your brother," the officer was saying.

"Oxygen – we need oxygen!" A medic was putting a mask over Mumma's face and they were carrying her out.

"Where are you taking her?" Aya's voice came out croaky, broken.

"We are going to look after her – and you too!"

Then Aya allowed herself to be helped out. She could barely stand and she would not let go of Moosa.

Outside, in a vast warehouse full of containers, Aya sat shivering, though they had wrapped her in a blanket made of what seemed like tinfoil. Still holding Moosa tight in her arms, refusing to let him go. She watched the medics helping people out. Some able to walk, some needing to be carried.

So this was Turkey. They had made it. Only not all of them. When Aya looked around she could not see the old lady.

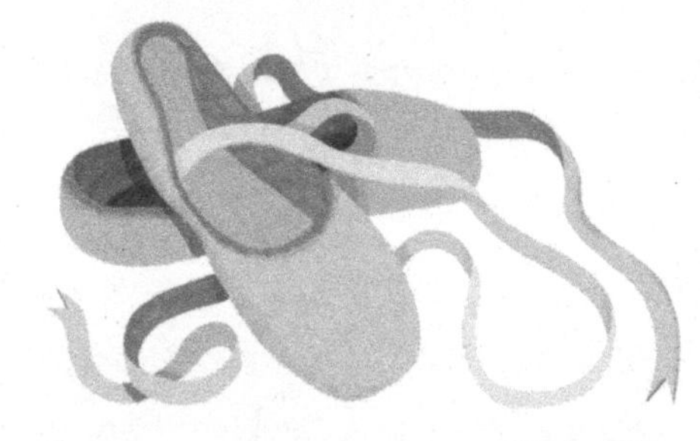

Chapter 25

They sat in the studio for what felt like an hour – but was perhaps only ten minutes – until eventually they heard the sound of voices outside and the door handle rattling. A jangle of keys. Miss Sylvie saying, "Why would you lock the door when the girls were still working in there?"

Aya was on her feet in an instant, rushing to the open door, flinging herself out – out into the lobby, her head still spinning with memories of the container, the dark, the airless blackness. The old lady who hadn't made it.

"I had no idea, honestly!" Ciara was saying to Miss Sylvie. "I thought they had gone home."

"You didn't think to, like, actually check?" said Dotty, who had appeared behind Aya now.

"The lights were off," said Ciara with a shrug. "I just assumed…"

Aya had closed her eyes and was trying to push away the memories of the darkness that were still spinning round her…

"Anyway, how was I supposed to know she would react like that?" Ciara was saying.

Aya knew how she must look. Like Mumma did sometimes. Pale, clammy, wild-eyed, washed-out. Damaged.

"It's OK. I'm OK," she managed to mutter. "I'm OK."

"When you flew at the door, I honestly thought you were going to bite your way out if you had to," said Dotty as they made their way downstairs.

"That is how I felt."

"I think maybe that's what Miss Helena means, you know," said Dotty. "About finding the most difficult places inside yourself and dancing from those."

Aya looked at her. She knew that her friend was right – she just had no idea how she was supposed to do it.

"That's why Ciara doesn't like you, an' all!" said Dotty, stopping and turning as she made her way in the direction of her mum's waiting car.

"Why?"

"Cos of the way you make people feel – when you dance. She's frightened of it. Just like you are of being closed in."

Aya wanted to ask her what she meant, but Bronte Buchanan sat in the front seat of the four-by-four and Aya caught her eye. She stopped. Dotty was pulling open the car door and saying, "Hi, Mum!"

Aya hung back and waved goodbye to Dotty, telling her she'd see her tomorrow, and then the car drove off and Aya was left on the pavement in the dark.

And when she got back to the bedsit, Mumma told her that they had to leave.

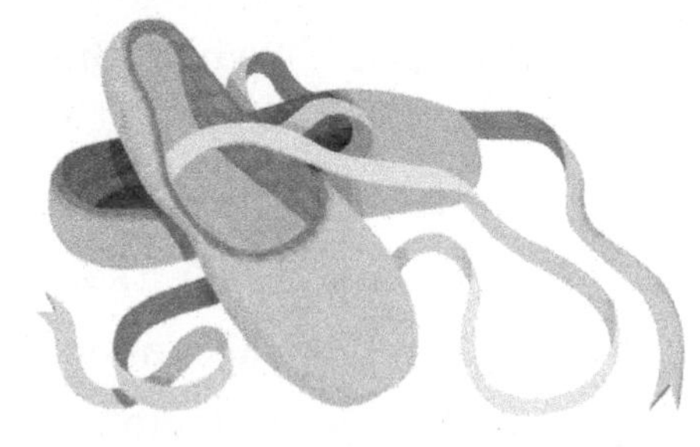

Chapter 26

When Miss Helena found Aya warming up in the studio the next day, her face was pale and her eyes ringed with dark circles.

"What is the matter?" asked the ballet teacher.

Aya recalled her mother's face when she had got home the previous night. The letter in her hand. "We have to move. Out of the bedsit. Away from Manchester."

Miss Helena's expression did not change. "When did you learn this?"

"Yesterday." Her voice sounded tight with the effort of trying to hold back the emotion.

The other girls had come in behind the dancing mistress and overheard what Aya had said.

Dotty looked horrified. "Why? But – no, they can't..."

"What about your dancing?" said Blue.

"Where will you go?" asked Lilli-Ella.

Aya could see her own pale face in the studio mirror. She felt the same awful sense of embarrassment and shame as when Dotty had offered her the hand-me-down clothes, but she tried hard not to show it.

"We don't have a choice," she said. "The landlord won't let us stay. It is the only place Sally can find for us."

"I'll talk to my mum ... my dad," said Dotty desperately. "I don't know – surely there's something we can do. To help, I mean."

"I will be back very shortly," said Miss Helena, speaking for the first time. "Warm up while you wait for me, please, ladies."

Class was temporarily abandoned, so the girls scattered around the floor, under the battered old barre, doing their stretches and questioning Aya. Ciara hadn't arrived yet and somehow the others were all more open, less self-conscious around Aya.

"I don't understand how they can just move you, just because you're a refugee," said Grace.

"We are asylum seekers – not refugees," said Aya,

flushing self-consciously as she tried to explain.

"Oh!" Blue's head popped up from a leg stretch. "Is there a difference?"

Aya remembered her father explaining it to her; it felt like a million years ago. In the camp in Kilis. Where they had to fill in forms, registering themselves as refugees. She hadn't understood and Dad had tried to explain what the different words meant.

"If you go to a new country because your home is too dangerous, then you ask for 'asylum'. It means a safe place."

"Right," said Dotty. "Then you are an asylum seeker – yes?"

Aya nodded. "And if a country agrees to let you stay – then you are a refugee."

"So actually you kind of want to be a refugee?" said Lilli-Ella. "It's a good thing?"

Aya nodded. Refugee meant safety, it meant staying, it meant a future.

"I never knew that's what it meant," said Blue. "I know that's dumb but…"

"I didn't know either," said Aya. "Before." She thought of all the things she had once known nothing of – bombs, and war, and homelessness, and fear. She was glad the others still knew nothing of them.

"So might you not be allowed to stay in England at all?" said Grace with a look of concern.

"Could they send you home?" asked Lilli-Ella.

"Maybe. It is complicated."

"How on earth is it complicated?" said Dotty, looking outraged. "Your home is a war zone. Where are you supposed to go?"

"Who decides this stuff anyway?" asked Blue, her stretches forgotten as she contemplated the injustice of the system.

"We have to go to the appeal," Aya said. "Soon. In court – with a judge."

"And do you have a lawyer?" asked Dotty.

"We have a caseworker but I don't think he's a lawyer." She shrugged her shoulders. They had no money for a lawyer, even if she knew who to ask.

Dotty looked troubled, her face twisted into a frown. "This can't be allowed to happen. You can't go away. You just can't."

Aya just looked at her. "We may not have a choice. People don't always have a choice."

Kilis Refugee Camp, Turkey

The Kilis refugee camp was their home all that winter. Just on the other side of the Turkish border from Syria, Kilis was a vast city of white containers, stretching in rows as far as the eye could see. Dad said there were over 13,000 refugees crowded into the camp – there were kindergartens, a makeshift school, a hospital. It was like a city but not a city. People survived here in a kind of limbo; unable to move forward, unable to go back home. The young, the strong – those who had the means – moved on from here. The rest – the elderly, the sick, the poor – sat outside the containers all day long, watching, waiting, existing – not living. Children ran up and down the brick rows that ran between the containers, kicking footballs fashioned out of plastic bags and playing with wire-hanger cars. It was safe, mostly – but it was not a home.

After they registered they were given cards that entitled them to rations from the food tent and other basic necessities. Dad tried to say it was like an adventure – a camping holiday. But Mumma hated it. She hated the airless container and the rows and rows of people, hundreds more arriving in the camp every day, streaming across the border like a river of the dispossessed. She hated living like beggars, stripped of all the things that made them feel human. She hated having to queue up for food and share meagre washing facilities with strangers.

"They frighten me," she said. "Their eyes – always staring. They look so empty."

Dad tried to reassure her. That this was only temporary. Until she was well enough to move again. Then they would get to England and find a new home, start a new life. And he held Mumma in his arms and told her to be brave – just for a little while – and everything would be OK again. They would find a proper home, he told her. "Everything will be OK," he said.

And then the winter came.

Aya would never forget the cold, the hunger, the sickness. Dad helped out in the camp hospital, where he dealt with cases of hypothermia and severe malnutrition as well as the many diseases that ran like wildfire through the overcrowded camp – typhoid, cholera, dysentery...

They were among the lucky ones. They had some money – not much because they had left in such a hurry – but enough to buy food on the black market in the town when supplies ran out in the camp, as they often did. And they had Dad to keep them well and safe. But still, when the snow fell and Moosa cried all night for the bitter cold, the only thing that kept Aya going was dancing.

She met a young woman in the camp called Rosarita who came from eastern Syria, who had trained with Madam Belova before setting up her own ballet school. Her town had been invaded by Isis forces and many people – including her husband – had been killed or kidnapped.

"I tell myself every day how lucky I was to get away," she told Aya.

"But ... your husband?"

"I have to think of the things I managed to save – as well as

those I lost," said Rosarita.

"How do you do that?"

"I have to fight against the current," she said with a smile. "The tide that would drag me always back into the past. I have to keep moving forward or I will be…" She hesitated. "Washed away."

Aya hadn't understood her at the time.

Rosarita ran dancing classes in the makeshift school tent for any children who were interested. It wasn't the same as training with Madam Belova. They had to use crates as barres and few of the children had shoes. Rosarita played music on an old iPod plugged into a tinny speaker. But it allowed Aya to maintain her flexibility and some of her skills. Sometimes she thought it was the only thing that helped her to survive that terrible winter.

When spring came, Mumma was still weak but well enough to travel. So they bought tickets for a bus that took them up through western Turkey. Aya sat next to her father, watching the road wind through villages and towns, over mountains and through rocky scrubland, and Dad had talked about the great future there would be for them in England.

"We will ride on double-decker buses, eat fish and chips, and have tea with the Queen!" he had laughed, pulling Aya close to him, the memories of the camp falling away as he spoke.

"With the Queen?"

"And all her corgis!" he added with a smile. "We can build

a new life there. A proper life. We will find you a dancing school and you will make new friends."

The only thing that Aya had been sad to say goodbye to at the camp was the dancing with Rosarita.

"A ballet school? Really?"

"The best ballet school in England!" Dad had laughed. "And our own house with a garden – the English like their gardens. They like pets too. Perhaps we will get a cat – or a goldfish!"

He had talked on and on like that, painting pictures of England that were daubed in bright colours across her mind, and she had laughed as he held her close, and dreamed of dancing again in a green English garden beneath sunny skies. Dancing across the grass of a new home.

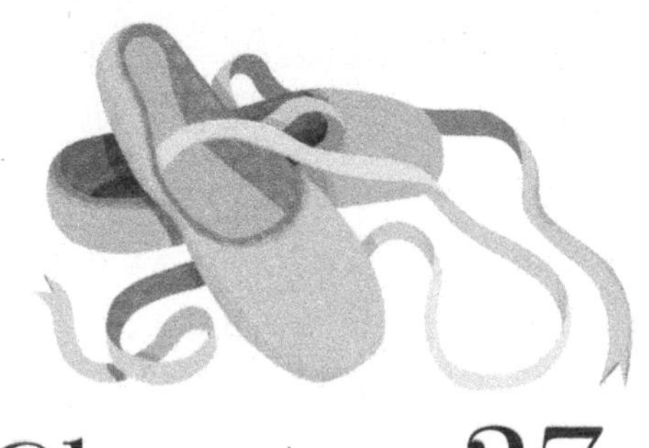

Chapter 27

Aya threw herself into preparing for the audition. What else could she do? Everything else was out of her control. They were going to have to move away in less than a week and then she had no idea how she would get to dance lessons, but she couldn't worry about that for now. All she could do was work as hard as she possibly could and hope they wouldn't move her away until after the audition. In class, she no longer paid attention to Ciara's snide comments, no longer even heard Dotty's sighs and groans, or the laughter of the other girls – she focused only on her own work. Miss Helena said it didn't matter that Aya had not been to the preliminary round of auditions. But Aya did not want to take that chance. She wanted to perfect every single move she could. To be as good as she could. To make this work.

Because if she passed the audition, then they couldn't send her back to Syria. That was what Dotty had said anyway. "I googled it – you can get a study visa. Then they'd have to let you stay."

"And my mumma? Moosa?"

Dotty scrunched up her face. "I'm not sure about them – my legalese isn't that good – but if you're here then surely it must be harder for the immigration people to throw your family out, right?"

"I suppose?" said Aya. She had no idea if Dotty was right; the caseworker just looked confused when she asked him. "I'm afraid ballet schools aren't something I normally deal with. Not really my area of expertise," he'd said. But if there was even a chance that Dotty could be right, then Aya had to pass the audition. She just had to.

Only, no matter how hard she worked, she couldn't seem to get her dance right. She worked on it with Miss Helena and with Dotty. She worked on it alone, out in the back yard, in the bedsit, in the empty studio. She even worked on it in bed at night, running through steps in her mind, trying to make the movements fit to the story, trying to make her body show where she had come from, what she had been through. But it never felt quite right. It felt … uncomfortable, and she couldn't lose herself in it as she did when she had danced back home.

She asked Miss Helena if she could devise a dance about something else – make up a story, not her own. That would be easier, she said.

"Easier, yes, but less honest. Less powerful," said Miss Helena. "The best dancing is not easy – to execute or to watch."

"But I can't seem to make it right," said Aya.

"Easy … Right… These are not words for a dancer," said Miss Helena. "These are words for a naughty boy doing his maths lesson. Maybe it will never be right, maybe it will always be difficult – but maybe that will make it more beautiful!"

"Maybe," said Aya. But the dance didn't feel beautiful – it felt awkward and stilted and no matter how hard she tried, she couldn't lose herself in it. And she feared that if she did, she might not ever find her way back again.

"I thought I'd pop in and watch one of the classes." The voice was low and lilting, coming from outside in the lobby when the girls were at the barre, just a couple of days before Aya and her family were due to be evicted. "If Miss Helena will allow me, that is?" Tinkling laughter and the smell of expensive perfume wafted through the door.

All the girls looked up and exchanged excited glances. Aya's heart started pounding hard in her chest.

"It would be wonderful to have you in the class, Bronte." This was Miss Sylvie speaking now. "I know all the girls will appreciate it."

Aya glanced at Dotty, who was staring at the door with an unreadable expression on her face. "State visit from my mother," she declared loudly.

"OMG!" said Lilli-Ella. "Bronte Buchanan is coming to our class!"

"Don't stress," said Dotty. "She won't find anything wrong with anyone other than me!"

Then the same lilting voice saying, "I've been so busy, with rehearsals for the new season and everything. I hardly feel I know how Dotty's audition prep is going."

Dotty groaned.

"And she's been talking so much about Aya." The voice was closer now. Light footsteps approaching the studio. "I confess, I'm intrigued!"

The other girls all turned to look at her. Aya realised her heart was pounding harder than ever and she felt slightly sick.

"Oh, I wish I'd sorted my hair out better," sighed Blue, whose orange curls were escaping wildly, defying all attempts to subdue them.

"And I wish I'd sorted my pirouettes," said Grace, rolling her eyes.

"Don't stress – she's just come to check up on the war child," said Ciara, and Aya felt herself flush even hotter. "She's been talking to my mum about bad influences … standards slipping…"

In any case, it was too late for anyone to sort anything, because just then Miss Helena entered the room, accompanied by a small, slender figure dressed in a neat grey trouser suit and red pumps with silver pom-poms on the toes. All the girls stood to attention and Aya could feel Bronte's eyes passing along the row before coming to rest on her.

"OK, girls, let us continue with our *battement jetés*."

Aya felt herself flush, but then she remembered Miss Helena saying, "England is a country of refugees – a country that once prided itself on helping the helpless." The words came back to Aya now as the music started and she lifted her eyes to meet those of Bronte Buchanan. "I have nothing to be ashamed of," she said to herself.

She tried to push away all thoughts except of dancing – keeping her shoulders level, her supporting leg turned out. Because, outside these doors, she was an asylum seeker, a would-be refugee, a poor little girl from Syria, a fatherless child from a war zone. But here, at the barre, in leotard and leather ballet shoes, she was like any other dancer. Dancing transcended borders; it cared nothing for languages, skin colour, nationality, religion. It did not require a passport. Or papers. Or "Leave to Remain". It could not be bombed, or shelled, or destroyed, or drowned. It was a safe space, but it was more than that. It was a timeless space, where wars and love and family existed and had always existed. It had been there before all this and would be there long after it was all gone.

She did not realise that she was dancing differently that day. That her thoughts flowed through her limbs, even when she was doing the simplest of movements. That her memories, her sadness, joy, melancholy, and her defiance – all of that was channelled through Aya's arms in the *port de bras*, through her extended leg in her *arabesque en fondu*, giving her a stronger, straighter composure, a more expressive tilt to her head, an intense light in her eyes that was magnetic and powerful beyond measure.

After the class was over, she curtsied to Miss Helena and to Bronte Buchanan, nervously lifting her eyes to meet those of the famous dancer, who was staring at her with a peculiar expression on her face. Bronte Buchanan held her gaze, inclined her head and smiled.

Then she turned to Miss Helena. "Now I understand," she said.

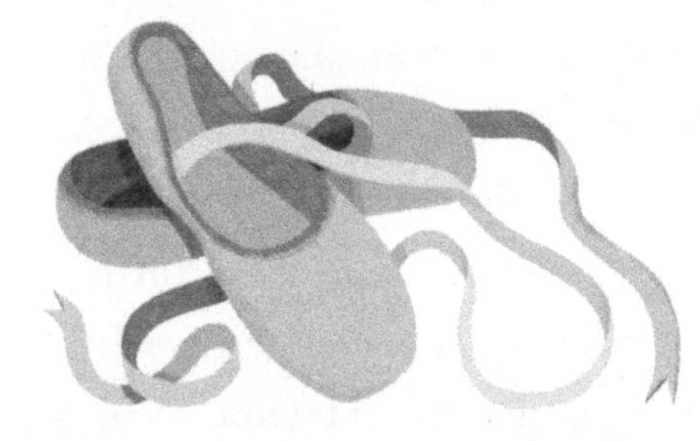

Chapter 28

"Thank you for letting me watch your class." As the girls pulled on jumpers and leggings in the lobby, Bronte Buchanan came over to talk to them all. "I was incredibly impressed – by all of you."

Ciara beamed as if the compliment had been for her alone.

"Lilli-Ella, your floor work is exquisite," she said. "Blue, I am so impressed by your lovely lines, and Grace, what an improvement in your *port de bras*!"

The three girls all looked thrilled with the compliments.

"Ciara, you are lovely, of course," smiled Bronte – causing Dotty to pull a face at Aya. "I just wonder if we could see a little more of what you are thinking – what you are feeling, as you dance?"

"That would NOT be a pretty picture!" Dotty muttered.

"Dotty." Bronte turned to her daughter now and Dotty flushed in a way that Aya had never seen before. Aya remembered the pleading expression on her face in her audition dance.

Then her mother smiled softly. "There is a difference in the way you move that I can't put my finger on, but I like it."

Dotty beamed. "Thanks," she managed to say.

"But you could manage to look as if you were enjoying it a little more!" Bronte added. "So many girls long for the opportunity you have."

Dotty's face fell and she looked as if she wanted to say something, but Bronte had already moved on.

"And Aya – it is Aya, isn't it?"

Aya nodded, feeling Bronte's eyes on her again. She could feel all the other girls watching her too.

"Aya, I hear you are auditioning for the Royal Northern," Bronte Buchanan was saying. In her flat red shoes she was tiny – Grace towered over her – and somehow not as scary as Aya had previously thought.

Aya nodded.

"Well, I wish you luck," said Bronte. "You deserve it."

"Thank you," Aya managed to say.

Bronte smiled and turned to her daughter. "Dotty, perhaps now your father is back from his business trip, Aya would like to come over to our house sometimes. You could practise together in the studio. That would be fun, wouldn't it?"

Dotty beamed some more. "Um, yes, that would be awesome! If – um – Aya would like to, that is?"

Bronte turned to her with an amused smile on her face. "Would you, Aya?"

Aya was staring at the ballerina. The way she stood, even the way she held her head had indescribable elegance and beauty.

"Yes..." she stammered. "Yes, I would."

"Perhaps this Saturday. After class?" Both girls nodded and Bronte smiled. "Good. Because sometimes I think we meet certain people for a reason. Now, I must go. Lovely to see you, girls. Oh, and, Dotty, your messy *jetés* are so much better than they were – but do keep working on them."

"Wow," said Dotty after she had gone. "How does my mother manage to make a compliment sound so … uncomplimentary!"

Izmir, Western Turkey

The sun was only just rising when they stepped off the bus but the port town was already bustling. They were immediately accosted by hawkers trying to sell them everything from sea-sickness pills to balloons to keep their valuables in. And others who crowded in, saying soft and low, "You are looking for a boat? I have a good boat. Very reliable. Take you and your family to Greece – no trouble." Aya hated the way they pressed round them – like birds of prey – and Moosa started to whimper.

Dad left them in a café in the town square while he went off to arrange it all. All around the square there were shops selling life jackets – blue, orange, red – wet bags, rubber inner tubes. There were signs offering "pre-crossing accommodation" and "migrant travel insurance". There was even a shop that sold police uniforms, with life jackets among the merchandise hanging out front. Refugees were big business in a town cashing in on the migrant crisis.

Dad came back a few hours later and took them to the single room they would stay in until the conditions were right to sail. There had been bad storms and the spring tides were not safe to cross just yet, he said.

"How long?" Mumma had asked.

"That depends on Allah's plans for the wind and weather!" Dad smiled. "Soon, I hope."

There were hundreds of families like theirs in the town. Some had been there for months, some stayed only a few weeks, more arrived every day. Mostly Syrian, all wanting to make the crossing to Greece to claim asylum in Europe. There was no future for anyone here, Dad said, because they could not get work permits. And going back wasn't an option.

Not everyone had enough money to pay the boat owners to get them across, so many people worked illegally to raise the fare, hawking cigarettes and alcohol in the town square, evading the Turkish police and customs officials. Aya made friends with a boy called Tariq whose family had been there nearly a year, selling trinkets in back streets to raise money for the crossing.

"Not everyone makes it," he told her. They were sitting in the town square. Aya had just been trying to teach him to do a grand jeté, *which had resulted in them both falling over in a heap on the floor.*

"What do you mean?"

"My dad says there are more Syrians under the sea than in the ruins of Aleppo," said Tariq with a shrug. He was ten years old but small for his age, with sharp black eyes like pebbles, and thin, wiry limbs.

"Well, my dad says it's worth the risk."

Tariq shrugged. "Just saying. I've seen the people they sent back. And heard their stories too."

"Sent back?"

"Yeah – some new agreement between the EU and Turkey," he said, tipping his chin up and sounding very superior, like he himself was a politician suddenly. "Even if you make it, they can still ship you back here if they catch you."

Aya surveyed him warily. He was tipping back and forth on his heels, pebble eyes twinkling.

"That's not true," said Aya. "Is it?"

"Ask your dad, he'll tell you!" said Tariq. "Come on – show me that jumpy thing again."

So Aya taught him how to stretch his leg when in the air, to make sure his head was moving in harmony with his body, to close quickly on landing. Tariq was a fast learner, she thought. He might have made a good dancer – maybe he still would. But for now he was selling trinkets to tourists in the streets.

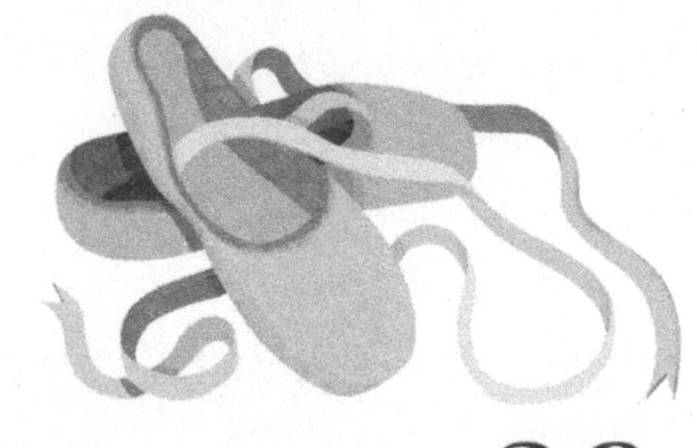

Chapter 29

Dotty's house was – well, it wasn't really a house, more like a mansion. "It's kind of embarrassing living in a place like this," Dotty said. "Like the Real Housewives of somewhere or other!"

Bronte Buchanan, who was driving them up the front drive, let out a tinkling laugh. "Dotty, you do say the silliest things."

"Oh, I know we're dead lucky but – well, after all Aya's been through. It makes you feel dead guilty about all this, to be honest!" Dotty waved a hand at the palatial mock-Tudor mansion, the sweeping driveway, the garage big enough to fit four cars.

"It's lovely," said Aya quietly.

"Seriously, Mum, I still don't get why Aya and her

family can't just come and live here with us."

Aya felt her stomach do a flip.

"Dotty, we talked about this..."

"But it would only be till they sorted things out," Dotty insisted. "And we have so much room."

Aya felt like she wanted to curl up on the back seat and die. It was like the time that Dotty had given her the clothes – only worse, because it was obvious that Bronte Buchanan hated the very idea of having a family of asylum seekers under her roof.

"Dotty, things are much more complicated than you realise," she said as they drew to a stop on the gravel in front of the house. "So can you please drop this!"

"It just doesn't seem fair, that's all," said Dotty.

"Please," said Aya. "It's OK."

She caught Bronte's eye in the rear-view mirror for a moment, then looked away quickly.

"Fine! This is my dad." Dotty was dragging Aya out of the car and introducing her to a tall man who had come out to greet them, with the same laughing eyes and dark-chocolate skin as Dotty. His hair was greying at the temples and he wore a sharp pin-striped business suit and old-fashioned-looking glasses that lent him a slightly boyish appearance. His smile was as wide as Dotty's as he clasped Aya's hand saying, "Ah! The famous Aya! I have heard so much about you from my daughter and my wife, I've been starting to feel a bit jealous!"

He laughed and Aya found it was impossible not to smile back. Mr Buchanan had a halo of warmth about him that reminded her of her own father somehow, and helped dispel the awkwardness that had engulfed her.

"Obviously, if you want to know anything about dancing, do ask me, as I believe I may be the most talented ballerina in the family!" As he said this, Mr Buchanan flung his arms in the air and executed a terribly clumsy spin that caused Dotty to groan loudly.

"Dad, you are *so* embarrassing!"

"What!" he exclaimed in mock surprise. "I danced *Swan Lake* with Nureyev, don't you know!"

"Come on, Aya. What do you want to see first, my room or the dance studio? Oh, dumb question. Come on!"

"Have fun – and don't forget to work on those *jetés*," Bronte called after them, but Dotty did not reply. "And I'll be taking Aya back at five, OK?"

Dotty's dance studio was in the conservatory, which

had been adapted specially, with sprung floors and a row of mirrors with a barre running alongside them. The walls were decorated with images of ballerinas, but when Aya looked closely, none of them was of Bronte herself. "Even mum reckons that training under her own watchful eye would be a bit intimidating!" Dotty laughed.

"Who's this?" Aya went up to one of the pictures of a young, dark-eyed dancer, *en attitude*.

"That's Miss Helena again," said Dotty. "She was lovely wasn't she?"

Aya nodded. The girl in the photo was young, possibly only early teens, and the date at the bottom read 15th July 1947. Miss Helena had said that she'd left her parents and her family when she was younger than Aya. During the war with Germany, many, many years ago. Had she ever seen them again, Aya wondered? And how did she keep on dancing without them? How did she keep training every day? How did she hold out against the tide?

"Come on, let's go and get a snack!" said Dotty. "A girl cannot live on ballet alone! And Miss Helena said we need to feed you up for the audition!"

The kitchen was a vast room, oceans of marble worktops, a white stone floor, and a giant pine table, with huge glass doors overlooking the garden.

"What was your house like?" Dotty asked as they sat down with milk and home-made cookies.

"Oh, it was an apartment," said Aya. The sun was shining through the glass doors, casting dappled sunny shadows on the table, reminding her of the late-summer sun in Aleppo.

"Sounds cool!" said Dotty.

"It was not as big as your house but it was nice – we had a roof terrace and we could see all of the city. And my dance school was very close." Aya had not talked to anyone about her home since she came here. It felt nice somehow to recall. "I could walk there by myself, before the war. Also it was near the hospital where my father worked. And near the park with the swimming pool – and the covered market..."

"Ooh – that gives me an idea!" Dotty jumped up excitedly. "I'll be right back!"

Then she was skipping out of the door, leaving Aya alone in the vast kitchen, remembering the view from the roof terrace, the castle towering over the city, the walk to school...

"Your father was a doctor, right?" Aya looked up to see that Mr Buchanan had come in and was standing with a cup of coffee by the counter.

"Oh – um – yes, he worked in England. In Birmingham."

"Really? Your mother didn't mention that."

"You've met my mum?" Aya looked surprised.

"Your Miss Helena is very good at making introductions." Dotty's dad grinned widely. "So do you know where your father worked? Or who he worked with?"

Dotty recalled the name of the consultant Dad had been in touch with and she told him. "And he worked with British doctors in the camp in Kilis too. Red Cross."

"I see," said Mr Buchanan thoughtfully. "That could be helpful, I suppose…"

"Helpful?" said Aya. She wanted to ask Mr Buchanan what he meant, why he wanted to know about Dad, why he'd been talking to her mother. But there was no time, because just then Dotty came bouncing into the kitchen with a giant grin on her face.

"Come on," said Dotty. "Let's go for a swim."

Izmir, Western Turkey

Moosa had never seen the ocean before. And Aya had only been to the seaside a few times – when she was younger, before the war started. She hardly remembered it, really. Moosa laughed and laughed when they dipped his toes in the waves. He had just started crawling by then, and he tried to put pebbles in his mouth while Dad showed Aya how to skim stones across the flat, white ocean that sparkled turquoise in the early-spring sunshine. Then they collected shells, picking out the ones with the best colours, the smoothest shapes. Dad picked up a shell and pressed it into her palm, pointing to the smudge of land on the horizon.

"See, it's not far away. Just a few miles across the sea. And then we are in Europe."

"Is it safe? In the boat?" She was thinking of what Tariq had said – about the people who didn't make it. Who lay at the bottom of the Med.

"Of course," said Dad.

"And if we get there, they can't send us back, can they?" She recalled Tariq's face as he'd said that – tipping back on his heels and offering it up like a challenge.

Dad's face creased into a frown. "They can, but I will not let that happen," he said.

"How?"

"I know people in the Red Cross – colleagues in England. They can't get me a visa or work in Turkey but once I am in Europe – well, people always need qualified doctors."

Aya glanced over to where Mumma was sitting with Moosa

by the rocks. It was a warm spring day but she was wrapped in a blanket. She was looking better though – better than she had for a long time, and she was laughing as she and Moosa played together. Dad glanced over in her direction then he turned back to Aya, his face serious now.

*"*Habibti,*" Dad said. "If anything happens – if we get separated ... if something goes wrong – you look after your Mumma, OK?"*

From his pocket he retrieved a plastic bag containing a wad of euros and a sheet of paper, covered in Dad's spidery, unreadable handwriting.

"Dad, I—"

Dad glanced over to Mumma again. "You look after each other," he said. "You go to England and I will meet you there, OK? There's money. And people who will help you – OK?"

"But, Dad—"

"It's just in case, habibti,*" said Dad, wrapping an arm round her and running his hand over her hair, his dark eyes softly serious as he spoke. "Just in case. Always better to plan for the worst and hope for the best – that's what I say!"*

Aya was still thinking of Tariq's stories – of capsized boats. Of the Greek authorities sending them back.

But Dad was smiling now, tossing a shell up and down in his palm. "Now, show me this new move you have been working on, where you hover in the air. Or the one where you jump like a cat." He smiled, his almond eyes reflecting the curling waves of the ocean.

"Dance for me, habibti.*"*

That was the last time she had danced for him.

Chapter 30

The world stopped for a second. Dotty was already on her feet, gulping down the last of her milk, stuffing another cookie in her mouth and making for the door.

"Didn't I say that we have a pool? It's outdoors, so we have to make use of the rare moments of sunshine we get here."

"But I..." Aya began to say. Her voice sounded distant – disconnected from herself – like the time they'd been locked in the studio. Only worse than that, even.

"Don't fret! I'll lend you a costume." Dotty was pulling her up from the table. "If we stay in any longer, Dad will never stop talking and you'll die of actual boredom. Come on!"

"Hey, young lady, I'll have you know that I am VERY interesting!" Mr Buchanan called out as they disappeared upstairs.

Aya wasn't aware of getting changed, of Dotty throwing different costumes at her, grabbing towels, Dotty talking non-stop. She barely took in Dotty's giant room, with the oceans of deep fluffy pink carpet, the bed hung with gauze like she was a princess, teddy bears and cuddly toys piled up and clothes scattered all over the floor and pouring out of the giant wardrobes.

She was aware of everything seeming brighter than usual, as memories lapped at the edges of her thoughts, like an ocean current that had ebbed briefly, but which rose now on the spring tides.

Then they were making their way down the staircase, along the marble hallway, out through the patio doors and across the warm paving stones.

Dotty was giggling but Aya's head felt empty, as if a distant wind was whistling through it. She could barely feel her legs and arms and when she looked up to the warm blue sky above, images etched themselves – words, phrases, the odd flash as of a photograph appearing somewhere in her blank brain. There for a moment – then gone again.

"Come on – race you!" Dotty was calling. She wore

a red swimming costume covered in white dots, and somewhere in Aya's brain she was aware of a rhyme playing: "Spotty – Dotty" as the dots swirled in front of her eyes.

Then Dotty was leaping, up through the air into the pool, and Aya felt panic rise. She closed her eyes and felt the wave overtake her.

Dotty's voice, somewhere far off: "Come on in! It's lovely and warm." But she seemed distant, as the tsunami of memories came, and there was no holding them back any more.

The Mediterranean Ocean

The boat they went in had been designed to hold no more than twelve, but there were thirty people squeezed into it. Grey, inflatable. The colour of the waves, Aya had thought when she saw it – not much bigger than the inflatables they played with at the water park in Aleppo. Before it was bombed, that is.

They left from a secluded beach at midnight so that the Turkish police would not see them. Minibuses bumping across the shingle, groups of people standing on the pebbly shore, their belongings tied into black bin bags. Babies in life jackets, crying. The men shouting at everyone that they had to hurry. Moosa screaming when the cold water hit him.

The waves had been choppy when they set off, heaving the tiny boat up and down on the swell so that Aya had thought she might be sick. But Dad had held her tight and told her a story – of a princess who went on a quest to a magical land, to escape from the dragon that had engulfed her home.

"She danced her way across the waves," he told her. "She danced over the mountains. Through the valleys. She danced till her slippers were rags..."

The winds picked up when they were out on open water. And then the boat seemed like a cat's plaything, being tossed about on the swell. People threw up. Aya recalled the sharp tang of vomit, the sting of sea salt in her eyes, Moosa's low terrified whimpers.

The man at the helm was yelling but Aya was too cold, too wet to hear what he was saying. She was shivering so hard and Dad was holding her so tight that her limbs hurt.

And then someone was in the water and there was screaming and people frantically trying to pull them back in. Then another wave hit and she was ripped from Dad's arms. There was blackness and confusion and she was in the water, gasping, rasping for breath calling out, "Dad! Dad!"

A flash of a blue life jacket and she could see Mumma but the boat was upturned and gone.

And there was no sign of Dad anywhere.

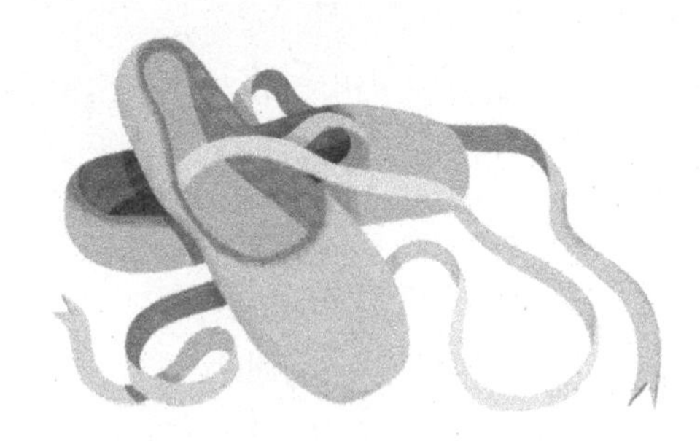

Chapter 31

"Aya! Aya! Are you OK?"

She didn't know how long she'd been standing there, staring. Somehow she was by the edge of the pool, outside, hot sun beating down on her. Blue tiling rippling in front of her eyes. Her body had gone into convulsive shivers. Dotty was wrapping a towel round her.

"Come on. Sit down. You're white as a sheet. Are you OK?"

Dotty was helping her to a sunlounger. "You're freezing cold," said Dotty. "What is it?"

"The water…" Aya managed to say. "The sea…"

Dotty sat down beside her. Though the hot sun was beating down, Aya shivered in the towel. Both girls sat staring at the turquoise-blue tiles, the patterns of the sun on the water, as Aya tried to find words.

"Were you on one of those boats? Like on the news. The migrant boats? My dad told me about them."

Aya nodded. "There was a storm … but my dad … He was in the water. We don't know…"

That was all she managed but Dotty seemed to understand. Both girls sat in silence for a moment.

"I'm sorry," said Dotty eventually. "I had no idea… I should have realised… I should have thought…"

Aya remembered the girl she had once been – dancing at Madam Belova's, walking hand in hand with Samia to school, even the girl who had watched the bombs fall over her home city. That girl would not have known of a world in which you leave your father out in the dark sea and never see him again. She would not have believed it possible.

"I mean, maybe your dad made it," said Dotty. "Maybe he got washed up somewhere. Or picked up by a boat, or…"

Dotty didn't finish. Aya shivered again. Sometimes the hope hurt so much it was worse than the grief. "Maybe," she said quickly.

"I read somewhere about the Red Cross and Amnesty – tracing missing people…" Dotty went on. "Maybe they can find him!"

"Maybe," Aya said again.

"All this stuff," Dotty said. "I'm sorry I haven't really got it before now."

Aya stared down at the slats on the wooden sunlounger, casting striped patterns on the tiling. "How could you?"

"But if you ever want to talk about it," said Dotty. "I mean, I know it's not easy to get a word in edgeways with me but, you know, I do know how to shut up – if I try really, really hard."

"It is hard to talk," said Aya, looking down at her bare feet on the slatted blue tiles. "Hard even to think some things."

"I get it," said Dotty. "I mean, I'm trying to, if that counts for anything."

"Thank you," said Aya. "Yes. It does."

That was when Bronte Buchanan reappeared. Wearing a crumpled old T-shirt over dusty leggings and a tattered pair of ballet shoes, she looked quite different to the elegant, aloof figure Aya had become used to seeing. She held a telephone in her hand. And she was smiling.

"Aya," she said. "That was Miss Helena on the phone. She has found you a home!"

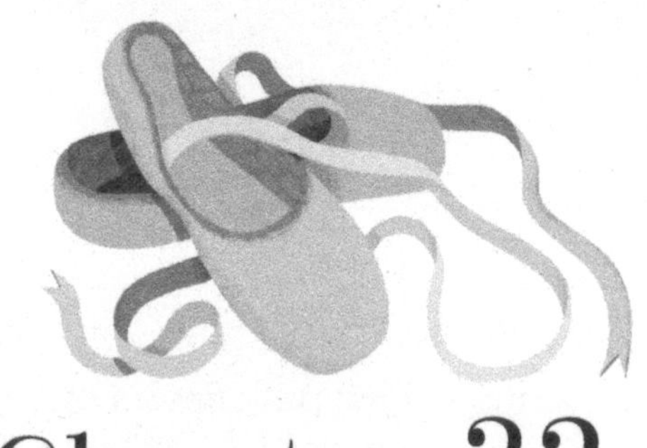

Chapter 32

Miss Helena and Miss Sylvie lived in a large Victorian villa. It was just a short walk from the community centre but felt as if it was in a different world. A world of tree-lined avenues, bay windows, glass extensions and double garages. Not that their house seemed to have been modernised – in fact, it didn't look as if it had been touched in over a hundred years. Red-brick and imposing, with a wildly overgrown garden and little turrets rising up over the grey-slate roof, surrounded by ancient beech trees, it reminded Aya for some reason of the story of the Sleeping Beauty in her forest-covered castle.

But when Miss Helena opened the door, Aya was met with the sweet smell of honey cake and pot-pourri.

The hallway was dark, decorated in old-fashioned floral wallpaper, with a wooden staircase, black-and-white tiling on the floor, and a stained-glass gaslight above the doorway that cast multicolours on to the walls and floor below. The house seemed to be frozen in time, but it had a warm, lived-in feel to it that felt more like home than anywhere Aya had been for months.

Miss Helena, it turned out, had offered to take them in as soon as she met Aya. But there had been paperwork, and safeguarding measures, and more paperwork. Sally had been making phone calls for days to try to fast-track it. But these things took time. Only now here they were. Aya was still trying to take it all in. To be offered a home. A place to stay … by people who still barely knew them.

"Let me show you to your room," said Miss Helena to Mumma, who was looking nervous and wary, hovering on the threshold. She took Mumma's arm and led her gently inside.

Miss Sylvie turned to Aya. "We thought you might like your own room. I hope that was right?"

Dotty – who had tagged along – replied for her. "Of course she would!"

"Thank you," said Aya again. She had lost count of how many times she had said it that day. The word had started to sound strange and unfamiliar on her own lips.

"Don't thank me till you see it," said Miss Sylvie with a wry smile. "It may not be to your taste!"

The room Aya was shown to looked as if it had once belonged to a little girl. There was a patchwork counterpane on the bed; wallpaper with roses fading on the walls; an ancient doll sitting on the dresser; a teddy bear with jointed limbs and a curious face staring at her from the bed. There were pictures on the wall too, black and white photos. One featured a medieval-looking bridge, with a castle towering behind it. The other was of a family, stiffly smiling, in clothes from a long-ago era.

"This was my mother's room when she was younger," said Miss Sylvie. "She thought you might like it."

Aya just nodded. It was hard to imagine having a bed all to herself. Space to call her own. Beautiful, interesting things to look at.

"Then I will leave you to settle in," said Miss Sylvie, who was always much more businesslike than her mother. "Dotty, you can come and help me make some tea."

Aya sat down on the bed. She could hear Miss Helena and Mumma laughing in the room next door.

It seemed like such a long time since she last heard her mother laugh.

She looked at the photo of the family on the wall. Her eyes traced the serious faces of the parents, then took in the older girl with long plaits who stood with her arm protectively round a little girl, whose eyes twinkled just like Miss Helena's.

Miss Helena never had told her what had happened to her family.

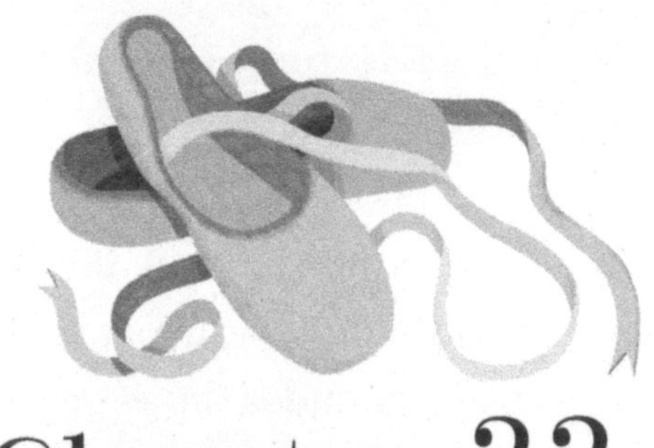

Chapter 33

"Maybe there have always been wars – always been refugees."

That night, after supper, Miss Helena told them her story. She sat in an old-fashioned armchair with a lace antimacassar on the back of it. Her usually bright eyes were clouded as she spoke, as if she were staring into the distance.

"Before the war my family lived in Prague, in what was then Czechoslovakia," she said. "We were prosperous. My father owned a store selling leather goods and my mother taught the piano. My sister Elsa and I went to a very nice school."

Aya thought of the older girl in the picture, with the serious face and long brown plaits. Elsa.

"This was the nineteen thirties and there had been much hardship but my family were well off," Miss Helena went on. Aya translated Miss Helena's words for her mother, who sat on the sofa with Moosa fast asleep in her lap. She had had a bath and her hair was clean and fluffy. She looked relaxed – tired, but relaxed.

"My sister Elsa and I attended ballet classes at the local seminary. We dreamed only of being dancers," Miss Helena said with a smile. "So we did not listen to the news on the radio, of the things that were happening across Europe. Hitler coming to power in Germany – the way that he was treating the Jews."

"You were Jewish?" asked Dotty, who was curled up on the sofa next to Aya, having persuaded her mum to let her stay for supper. She hadn't spoken up till now. Aya wondered if it was the longest she had stayed quiet in her whole life.

"I didn't think of myself as religious," said Miss Helena. "My family celebrated Yom Kippur and Chanukah but my parents were not Orthodox Jews. It was just a way of life. Tradition, I suppose."

Miss Sylvie sat in the chair next to her mother, darning the pointes of a pair of ballet shoes, and she looked up only occasionally as Miss Helena spoke. An old grandfather clock in the corner ticked loudly in the background.

"There were rumours … of the Germans invading Czechoslovakia," Miss Helena was saying. "My mother started to talk of leaving, trying to get papers to go to England, America, Australia. But my father said the English would never allow Hitler to march into Prague." She paused. "It turned out he was wrong."

As she translated the old lady's words as best she could, Aya thought how Miss Helena's story echoed her own. How it echoed so many families' stories in so many cities in so many different times, told in so many different languages.

"In March 1939, the Nazis took Prague," Miss Helena went on. The words were coming quicker now and she didn't always stop for Aya to translate. "We saw them march across the Charles Bridge. I remember it well – the day Hitler spoke to his troops from the castle as if he were king of all the land."

Aya recalled the picture in her room. The bridge, the castle.

"After the Germans came, *then* I knew I was a Jew," Miss Helena said, nodding her head emphatically. "And I knew – young as I was – that it was a dangerous thing to be."

Aya stopped translating now and just allowed Miss

Helena to speak. There would be time for explanations later. "My father's business was taken away. My mother was no longer allowed to teach..."

Her voice cracked and Miss Sylvie reached out and put her hand on her mother's.

"We were forced to wear yellow stars. My sister and I could no longer attend our school. Or go to our dance lessons." She paused, eyes glimmering now in the soft lamplight.

"There were many arrests, many taken away." Miss Sylvie spoke now, taking up the story for her mother. "It was no longer safe for my mother's family to stay."

"So you left?" Dotty asked.

Miss Helena shook her head sadly. "It was too late by then for the whole family. But there was an organisation taking children – the Kindertransport, it was called..."

Miss Helena's voice cracked again and her daughter went on while the older woman closed her eyes and listened.

"Many British families agreed to take in children," Miss Sylvie explained. "They did not know how long for. Some thought that Hitler would be driven out quickly. Gone by Christmas. Nobody saw what he would actually do."

Aya remembered her father and his friends sitting in

the kitchen, talking about the war in Syria. Some had said it would burn itself out in a few months. That the president would be toppled by Christmas and peace restored. Nobody had predicted how long it would last. How much would be lost.

"So you and your sister...?" Aya looked at Miss Helena, whose eyes were open now, and very bright in the lamplight.

"Just me," said Miss Helena. The clock ticked on for second after second and nobody spoke.

"I came here to this house in August 1939," said Miss Helena eventually, her voice businesslike again. "I was younger than you are now – just six years old. Mr and Mrs Robertson were in their fifties. They had lost their only son to tuberculosis and they said they had room in their hearts for another child."

"My mother was very fortunate," said Miss Sylvie. "Not every child who came had such a warm welcome. She was given a new family, a new start here."

Aya wanted to ask about her mother, her father ... and Elsa.

But Miss Helena looked tired and Miss Sylvie smiled and picked up the ballet shoe she had been darning. "My mother and I want you to know that you are welcome to stay as long as you wish."

Mumma seemed to understand this last bit. She thanked them with tears in her eyes and Aya translated her mother's words for Miss Helena and Miss Sylvie, but all the time she was thinking of the little girl who had come here alone, all those years ago, leaving her family behind. The little girl who had slept in the room that was now hers.

Had she ever seen her parents – her sister – again?

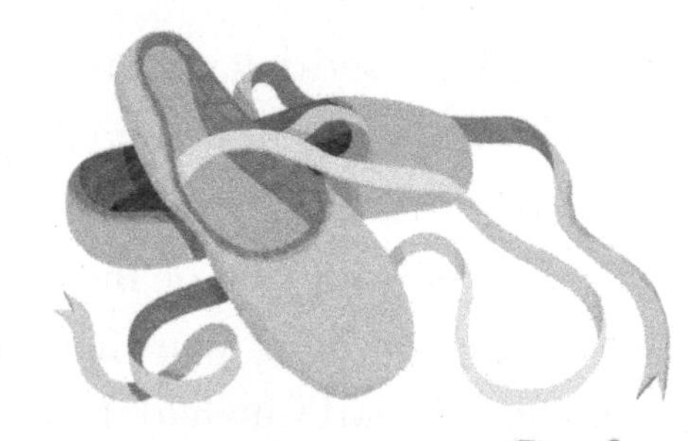

Chapter 34

That night Aya lay in the narrow bed, listening to the sound of the rain on the windowpanes. It felt strange to be sleeping alone – without Moosa curled up next to her, his warm little body and snotty kisses and little fingers that curled themselves round hers in the night. In the gloom, Aya stared at the family picture on the wall. There they were – two young girls with their parents, laughing at the camera, the elder sister with her arm round the younger one. It was dated May 1938. A year before the war started.

A few notes of music trickled through Aya's mind. She imagined dancing a few steps, linking together movements that seemed to come to her unbidden – something to do with Miss Helena's story, something of her own.

She lay like that for a long time, dancing through the notes in her head, watching the shadows from the street lamp and the passing cars make patterns on the curtains. But still she could not sleep. It was hard not to think of Dad. Of the last time she had seen him. And of Mumma and Moosa asleep in the next room. The thoughts seemed to come together like a dance.

The next morning when Miss Sylvie came to wake her, she found the bed empty. And when she looked in next door, she saw that Aya had tiptoed into her mother's room and lay curled up with Moosa held tight in her arms.

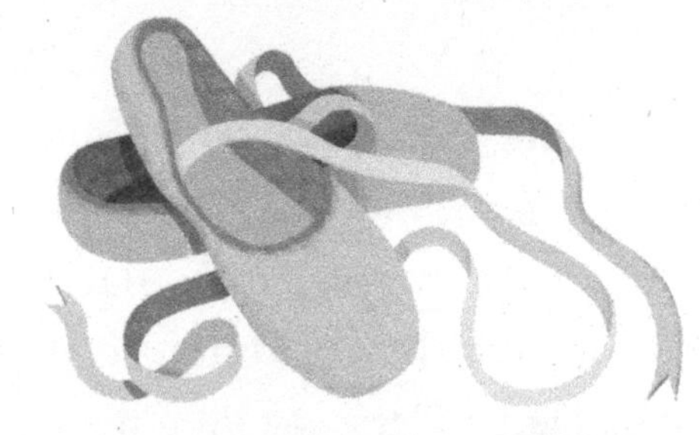

Chapter 35

The temperatures soared over the next week and Aya started, little by little, to feel different – a little lighter, a little less anxious. Living with the two ballet mistresses, growing healthy on the good food they insisted on her eating, dancing every day, spending time at Dotty's house, practising in her studio or going for long walks in the woods that surrounded the Buchanans' home, playing with Moosa in the garden under the giant old beech trees… It was nice to be just a big sister. Nice not to feel always responsible for Mumma. To play. To laugh. She still woke up with the yawning ache in her stomach every morning when she thought about Dad, but the pulse of anxiety that had hammered in her head ever since that night in the ocean beat a little quieter, and sometimes – when she was dancing – she could forget about it altogether, just for a short while.

And that difference started to creep into her dancing. As she worked on her audition dance, she felt a little more able to connect with the objects and open up the feelings they tugged at within her. She couldn't let it all out – that still felt impossible somehow – but she could start to tell some of the story, some of her fear, some of her homesickness, some of the hopes and dreams. It still wasn't right, but bits of it felt better somehow.

"This dance is starting to be beautiful," said Miss Helena when Aya showed her what she had been working on. "Sad and lovely and hopeful, all at the same time. And, Dotty, your work is much improved too. There is more compassion in it, more warmth."

Dotty beamed. "I found myself thinking about Aya. And how I'm lucky to have both my parents around – even if they are super annoying at times." She shrugged.

Dotty had also been working on a plan of her own. She'd been talking to her dad and to Sally and she'd come up with the idea of putting on a gala show to raise money for the refugee centre.

"Every single kid from the ballet school could perform," she explained. "And Mum said she'd do a star turn. We'd sell tickets and do a raffle for charity.

There'll be cakes and all that other stuff that always raises loads of money!"

"This is a wonderful thing!" said Aya.

"We'll be raising money for stuff the centre needs – and have great fun at the same time!"

It wasn't just ballet she had in mind either. "I thought Mr Abdul could do a tap number. Blue and Grace, you could accompany him – because you do tap, don't you?" she said, when she was explaining the idea to the other girls.

Blue and Grace looked at each other a little uncertainly. "Um – yes. I suppose we could."

"And Lilli-Ella, I thought you and me could do a bit of a ballroom mash-up with help from Mrs Massoud – maybe with a bit of hip-hop? What do you think?"

Lilli-Ella grinned a little nervously. "You think that would work?"

"Yes, and me and Aya are going to teach the little ones a number from *Cats*, and they can all wear little ears and tails," Dotty went on excitedly. "And I thought we could all do a ballet piece. And me and Aya and Ciara can do our audition dances. Right, Ciara?"

Aya glanced at Ciara, who had said nothing until now. The other girls had been much friendlier recently but things were always different when Ciara was around.

She had been acting even more cold and uptight than usual lately, and Aya wondered if she was more stressed than she let on.

"I've got the most important audition of my life coming up," Ciara shrugged. "I don't have time to be playing at putting on shows."

"This isn't just about the show though," Blue said, glancing awkwardly from Ciara to Aya, as if she felt she had to take sides.

"Yeah," said Lilli-Ella, coming to her aid. "It's to raise money. For asylum seekers like Aya and her family."

"To help pay for a proper lawyer," added Grace, ignoring the scowl on Ciara's face. "And medical stuff – and food and clothes and everything."

"Whatever. If you girls want to mess around putting on a silly show, go ahead!" said Ciara. "But count me out."

She stormed into the studio, slamming the door dramatically behind her. For what felt like forever nobody said anything. It was Blue who broke the silence.

"Aya, my mum showed me this article about refugees and the terrible journeys they have been on to get to England," she said. "Was it like that for you?"

Aya glanced at Dotty. She hadn't told the others

about the journey in the container, the boat. "I—"

"We're also raising money for a counsellor," Dotty cut in quickly, shooting Blue a warning look. "Because a lot of the people who have come here have had traumatic experiences that they find hard to talk about."

Aya glanced at her gratefully, and fortunately at that moment Miss Sylvie appeared.

"Girls – to the barre, enough chat!" Miss Sylvie's voice was crisp and curt.

"If Ciara doesn't want to perform, that's fine," Dotty said, linking arms with Aya and grinning at the others. "We can get this show on the road without her – and it's going to be awesome!"

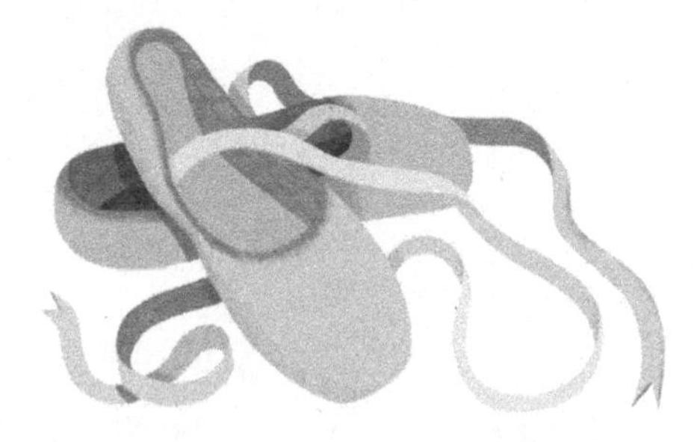

Chapter 36

"We did a gala at Madam Belova's one time," said Aya.

She and Dotty were out in Miss Helena's overgrown back garden, making a dozen cat tails out of old socks and the contents of a moth-eaten eiderdown. The sun was shining through the beech trees, casting dappled light on the small space of lawn and making the red brick of the Victorian villa glow almost crimson.

"Ooh, what did you do?" said Dotty.

Lately Aya had found herself telling Dotty more and more tales of home. Not the sad ones – just the stories of her ordinary life: school, parties, shopping, sports days, dancing lessons. Not so different from Dotty's life – not really.

"I did a dance with my friends – Kimi, and Nadiya and Nooda," she smiled. "And Samia! She was a lot like you."

"Poor her! So how was it?"

"Samia, she stumbled and fell off the stage." Aya smiled as she remembered how everyone had gasped and then a second later Samia had popped her head up with a giant grin on her face. "She got the biggest cheer of the whole show!"

She remembered Samia looking up, eyes wide with shock just for a second, and then the audience erupted into laughter and Samia was on her feet, clowning and playing along, as if it had all been part of the performance. Aya and the others had to try to carry on with the dance through their own giggles. So much had happened to her friends since then. She didn't know if she'd ever see Samia again but that was the version of Samia that Aya wanted to remember.

That was when Mumma appeared by the patio doorway. Aya had left Mumma with Miss Sylvie, cooking in the old big kitchen. Mumma had been teaching Miss Sylvie how to make *manoushi* bread, the two women somehow communicating in a mixture of gestures and the few words of each other's languages they had managed to glean, while Moosa made a nuisance of himself sticking fingers in the dough. Both women had been laughing when Aya left them, but now Mumma was holding a letter and she looked different somehow.

"What is it?" Aya was on her feet, crossing the grass, taking Mumma's hand.

Mumma said nothing. She'd also changed since they'd come to live with Miss Sylvie and Miss Helena. She'd been eating and sleeping better, and her hair and skin had regained some of their shine. Miss Helena had taken her to the doctor who had given her some pills and referred her to a counsellor. Her eyes still looked tired – and a little blank somehow – but the dark shadows under them were less pronounced than they had been. But now she looked frantic, more anxious than Aya had ever seen her.

"The hearing. The asylum appeal. It is next week."

She handed Aya the letter. Dotty was beside her in an instant, reading it over her shoulder.

"This is good news, right?"

"I don't know," said Aya.

"Course it is! After the appeal, everything will be sorted. You'll be able to stay forever!" said Dotty.

The sun suddenly felt too hot on her back, the light too bright. "Only if we win," Aya said. "If we lose, they will send us back."

"Then you can't lose!" said Dotty. "When is it anyway?"

That was when Aya looked properly at the date on the letter. "Next Tuesday," she said.

Then she looked at Dotty in horror.

The day of the audition.

Souda Refugee Camp, Chios Island, Greece

Aya remembered sitting on the pebbly beach, staring out at the blue smudge where the water hit the horizon. Her hands were bleeding again – fresh red coming through the darkened bandage where the boat's ropes had burned through her skin during that long, long night on the ocean before the rescue boat turned up – but she scarcely noticed. Her eyes were constantly scanning the horizon. Looking for Dad. Waiting for Dad. Praying and hoping for Dad.

She sat there on the beach all day, every day. But he never came.

After the rescue boat arrived, they had been taken to the Souda refugee camp on the island of Chios. It wasn't an official camp – just a makeshift settlement that had sprung up next to the ruins of an ancient castle, overcrowded tents pitched on the edge of the pebbled shore, rats roaming among the garbage. There were over three thousand refugees living here, mostly from Afghanistan, Syria and Iraq. It was not safe to go out after dark. Aya had started covering her head because of the way some of the men looked at her. At night, in the tent, they often heard shouts and screams that made it hard to sleep. And in the day there was nothing to do but stare at the sea.

Everyone here was waiting to be granted asylum, or to be assigned a relocation country. A translator in the overcrowded help centre had tried to explain to them that as a single mother with children, Mumma could claim protected refugee status, apply for asylum in Greece. But Mumma had just shut down by then, stopped talking. She didn't cry. She just sat, silent, all the time.

"But then can we go to England?" Aya was the family spokesperson now.

"You can't apply for asylum in more than one EU country."

Aya tried to remember what her dad had told her but it all seemed muddled in her brain. The money, the paper with the names – everything had been lost. "My dad said to meet him in England…"

The aid worker was young, with red hair pulled back into a messy ponytail. She spoke Arabic with a strange lisp and her eyes were different colours – one blue, one brown. Her name was Ezi – Aya remembered that for some reason.

"Aya, your father…" she started to say. "He was out at sea for over twelve hours. We have no reports of any other rescue ships…"

Aya stared hard at the young woman's one blue eye, the colour of the water, the sky.

"Dad said he would meet us in England," she repeated quietly. "So we have to go there."

She could hear Dad's voice in her memory telling her: "If anything happens to me – if we get separated, you take your Mumma and Moos and you go to England, OK?"

Ezi looked at her, her mismatched eyes full of concern. "Aya, your father…"

She didn't finish her sentence. And anyway, Aya wasn't sure she could do it. Not on her own. And maybe Dad would come. Maybe if she waited – and watched – just a little bit longer… maybe he would come.

Chapter 37

It was one of those mornings that felt like the last day of summer. The sun woke Aya hours before the rest of the house was up, pouring through the curtains, spilling over the bed, blazingly bright.

"As if the sun is saying goodbye," said Aya when Dotty came to pick her up after breakfast. She'd had that feeling for days now. As if she was saying goodbye to people, places, things that she had come to love and which she might never see again after today.

"What a funny thing to say," said Dotty, whose hair was pulled back into a bun so severe it made her whole face look different – more serious somehow. "But then today is a funny old day. I can't decide if I feel sick with nerves or just relieved it's finally going to be over. At least we get to know one way or another now."

"Yes," said Aya, but she was thinking as much about the appeal as the audition.

Sally and Miss Sylvie and Dotty's mum and dad were both going to the hearing with Mumma. "To give character references – say what a nice family you are – help your mum explain stuff right," said Dotty. "Oh, and Mum's going to work the celebrity angle. '*Famous ballerina fights for young refugee dancer and her family to stay in the UK*', and all that!" Dotty grinned. "She's got newspapers coming and everything."

"Really?" said Aya.

She felt almost overwhelmed by everything people were doing for her and her family. The kindness of strangers, Miss Helena had called it. Sometimes it made her want to cry more than the cruelty she had seen, though she could not explain why. And it made it all the more important not to let them down.

"And did you tell her – your mum – that you want to do musical theatre, not ballet?" Aya asked. Dotty had been saying for the past week that she was just going to tell her mum once and for all.

She'd been preparing a musical theatre medley for the show. "It makes me feel like I can see you do when you dance," she had told Aya. "And I want to feel that way all the time."

"So did you tell her?"

"No point," said Dotty. "She kissed me this morning and told me to enjoy 'the best day of my life'!" She gave an ironic grin. "What exactly am I supposed to say to that!"

Mumma wanted to do her hair for the audition, just as she used to back in Aleppo when Aya was little, and so after breakfast Aya sat in front of the old dressing table, staring at her own reflection as Mumma ran the brush through her brown locks. Neither of them said anything. Through the window Aya could see the tall trees that towered over Miss Helena and Miss Sylvie's house. How old were those trees, she wondered? Miss Helena said they had been nearly as tall when she had come here as a girl, eighty years earlier. How many wars had been fought while these trees grew? How many thousands of families driven from their homes, fleeing conflict, seeking refuge in faraway lands? Their story was hardly unique. They were one family among thousands. Why should they be allowed to stay? Why should anyone care?

"There," said Mumma, when Aya's hair was ready, pinned tightly into a bun, swept back off her face so that it accentuated the dark of her eyes, making them look huge in her pale face.

Aya reached up and took her hand. Mumma squeezed her fingers tight. "You look beautiful, *habibti*," Mumma said. "My beautiful *balletka*. My beautiful dancer."

Miss Sylvie drove the girls to the audition in an old-fashioned Morris Minor that looked as if it had spent most of its life under dust sheets in the garage. They drove out of the city, through giant concrete underpasses, past the towering edifice of the football stadium, and the new red pavilions in the old cricket ground, through rows of terraces, then out into the suburbs and finally the surrounding countryside.

"Remember also to enjoy yourselves, yes?" said Miss Helena as they drew near to the school.

"Flipping heck!" Dotty whispered. "It's bad enough that we have to survive this ordeal, without being expected to enjoy it now too!"

Aya tried to smile. Today was too important to worry about enjoying herself.

The Royal Northern Ballet School was accessed via a pair of imposing-looking gates and then up a long drive that seemed to last forever. Aya had seen pictures in the brochure, but she was still overwhelmed.

"Did you ever come across a school that had its own

deer park?" laughed Dotty.

The sun beat down relentlessly and as they turned the corner and saw the rich red-brick stately home, it seemed to glow coppery like sunset. Aya felt her heart beat hard in her chest at the thought of dancing every day in this beautiful, magical place. She tried to push the feeling away, train herself not to hope, because hope hurt so much when it was shattered. And how could she come here anyway, if Mumma and Moosa were sent away?

"Come on!" said Dotty, dragging Aya out of the car. "Let's get this over and done with!"

Inside was shabbier than the outside suggested. The entrance hall was grand but battered, the paintwork scuffed by generations of young ballerinas who had bustled through the hallways and up and down the staircases, scuffing their feet across the wooden floorboards and leaving the carpets threadbare. It smelled a bit like the refugee centre, Aya thought. That same mixture of sweat and school dinners – but without the smell of sadness.

The two girls stood in the entrance hall, clutching ballet shoes and music, while a severe-looking receptionist ticked them off on her list. There were a dozen or so other girls, all about their age, all waiting, looking pale and nervous. And Ciara was there, of course, looking immaculate and utterly composed next to a woman who must be her mother. Aya realised she had never seen Ciara's mother before. She was a small, anxious-looking woman, as plain as her daughter was beautiful, and with slightly sloping shoulders and a shy smile, which she turned to Aya and Dotty.

"It's lovely to meet you girls," she said. "Ciara is always talking about her friends from ballet."

"Really?!" said Dotty, glancing at Ciara, who would not meet her eye.

"Yes, she's never been very lucky with friends at school," Ciara's mum went on, a little nervously. Ciara flushed bright red. "So her dance pals are so important to her."

Dotty opened her eyes wide and looked as if she was about to say something, but Ciara was looking so uncomfortable that Dotty closed her mouth in surprise.

It was Aya who said, "They have all been very kind to me also."

Ciara shot her what seemed like a grateful glance, then looked quickly away.

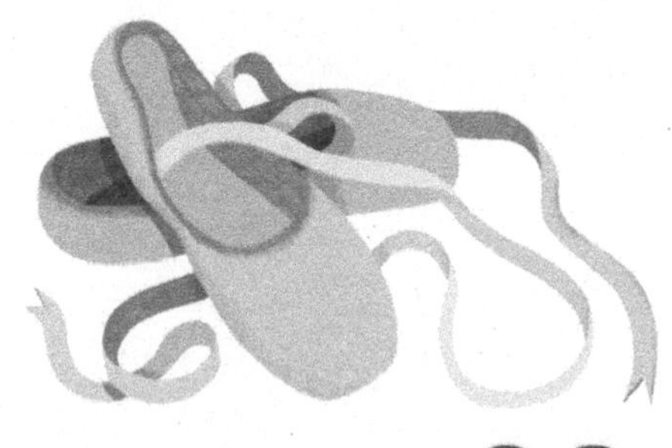

Chapter 38

There was a nervous wait in the lobby. Most of the girls were talking about ballet, adjusting their shoes, smoothing down their hair, but Aya couldn't stop thinking about Mumma, sitting in a waiting room like this, outside the courtroom. The hearing was at midday but Sally said they often ran late.

"I just need to use the bathroom," she said to Dotty.

She made her way to the bathroom and was hurrying back when she overheard Miss Helena's voice. She was talking to someone on the telephone further down the corridor. Aya didn't mean to eavesdrop but she couldn't help overhearing.

"...such a shame about the timing," she was saying. "If Aya had a place at the Royal Northern it would have really helped the case…"

Aya froze.

Miss Helena went on. "…I won't tell her yet. At least this way she has a chance to audition before they are deported. And maybe she can apply for a study visa. That won't help her mother and Moosa, of course…"

Aya did not stay to listen to any more. She ran back down the corridor, back to the lobby, her head bursting as she pushed her way back into the waiting room, where a young woman with old-fashioned clothes was calling out their names. There was no time to stop and think, no time to find Miss Helena to ask what she had meant. Were they being deported? Had they lost the appeal?

She and all the girls were being ushered into a large room with high windows, mirrors and a barre running round three sides. Dappled light fell on to the wooden floorboards, and Aya found herself staring at the play of shadow and light on the floor, her head running over the conversation she had just heard as the teacher addressed the class.

"I am Miss Eve," she was saying. She was young, early twenties perhaps, but with a streak of silver in her red hair and clothes that seemed to come from another era. "I will be taking the class today while my colleagues observe."

She waved to a desk at the far end of the room, where there sat a man with a bald head, small moustache and an alarmingly large bow tie, and an elegantly dressed older lady with violet-coloured hair cut into a stylish bob. Aya stared at them blankly, her mind still racing.

"Mr Bougeard, our principal ballet master, and Madam Olenska, director of the school."

Aya thought they looked like judges in a court room. Her stomach twisted sharply.

"At least this way she has a chance to audition before they are deported."

Miss Eve was explaining that this would just be like an ordinary class. "Just try your best, as you would in your own dance schools," she was saying.

Aya stared at her. With her flaming-red hair, she reminded Aya of the helper in the refugee centre in Souda. The one with different-coloured eyes. Suddenly Aya could not remember her name – all she could think of was the young woman saying, *"He was out at sea for over twelve hours. We have no reports of other rescue ships…"*

She felt hot, dizzy, hardly able to breathe – so many different feelings swirling around in her.

"We are looking for potential, so don't worry if you can't do everything," Miss Eve was saying. "Just do what you can and – try to enjoy it!" She smiled.

The music started then. Or had it started a few seconds earlier? Aya began late, a moment behind the beat, missing her footwork, feeling herself colour hotly.

"Maybe she can apply for a study visa – though that won't help her mother and Moosa, of course."

Things didn't go well. She tried hard to focus on the class, to concentrate on her hands, her feet, her fingers, the lines she was making with her body, pointing her toes, holding her chin up – but her mind kept wandering, dancing skittishly, and her body seemed unable or unwilling to obey. The room was close and airless and she could smell the scents of England outside – sweet summer smells of grass and flowers and Miss Helena's garden. Yet thoughts of Aleppo kept filling her head – the first night of the bombing, the sound of the call to prayer … the blood running down her leg in the dust-filled street.

Miss Eve was walking up and down. The other two teachers sat making notes behind the desk. Aya couldn't seem to pull her mind into focus, couldn't even seem to hear the beat of the music properly. Other sounds and sights seemed to cloud her head – the old woman in the container, children dying of cold in the camp in Kilis…

They were moving to the centre now. Dotty was

saying something to her as they dipped their feet in rosin to keep their shoes from slipping.

"Are you OK?" she whispered.

Aya tried to nod but wasn't sure if her head obeyed the command. She felt like Mumma, adrift from time and place, unanchored, floating free and not able to grasp hold of the moment. *Her* moment – this was her chance, everyone had said. But what did the chance mean if it was too late to help Mumma and Moosa anyway? She had promised Dad she would look after them; she couldn't leave them.

"We want to see your *port de bras*, ladies," Miss Eve was saying. "Nothing too complicated, but we are looking for excellence in every move."

Out of the corner of her eye, Aya could see Ciara, caught in a shaft of sunlight. She seemed to glow like an angel, but her face was tight with concentration and anxiety. She was tense like Aya had never seen her and she kept making mistakes. Aya had never seen that either. To her other side, she was aware of Dotty, her face screwed up with effort. She fumbled a couple of moves and Aya could see her bite her lip hard.

The music continued to play as they moved to floor exercises – jumps and leaps, moving from one corner of the room to another. Then arabesques … pirouettes … Aya moved on autopilot – the heat, the warm notes mingling with the smell of the grass, the images in her head … of her old classmates – Samia falling off the stage, the twins dancing their mirror dance on the rooftop of her house, Kimi bent over Ifima's lifeless body in the street. Where were they all now? Scattered across the globe – who knew where? Had any of them made it? Were any of them even alive? Why did she get this chance? How could she keep dancing when so many others were still suffering?

Then the class was over and she was barely aware of how it had gone or what she had been doing. All she could think of were Miss Helena's words. *"If Aya had a place at the Royal Northern it would have really helped the case."*

But it was too late – she was too late. And now it was all over.

"How did it go?" asked Dotty as they made their way out into the corridor after final curtseys.

Aya turned to her blankly. "I… I don't really know."

"I got in a right pickle with those final floor combinations," Dotty was saying. "But I don't think I disgraced myself at the barre."

Aya tried to remember the floor work, but could only retain a sketchy memory of Miss Eve talking through steps she could barely remember doing.

"I went to pieces at the barre," said Ciara who was pale and tearful-looking. "And everyone here is so good!"

Aya said nothing. She hadn't noticed how the other girls had danced. She hadn't noticed anything.

"Are you OK?" asked Dotty, looking at her anxiously.

"Yes – I … don't know."

"Are you worrying about your mum?"

Aya nodded.

"She would want you to think about yourself today," said Dotty. "This is your moment. Remember?"

But Aya felt as if the moment was slipping away from her. As if she were being dragged back on a current she couldn't resist. And she didn't even know if she wanted to fight it any more.

Chapter 39

The girls were ushered into a small room where they would wait to be called in for their individual assessments. Some were discussing the class, nervously. Others – like Aya – sat quietly. Each girl in turn was invited back into the studio before the panel of judges for an interview. Dotty was one of the first to go, Aya one of the last. She didn't know if there was any point in her completing the audition, but she didn't want to let Miss Helena down.

So when her name was finally called, she made her way back into the dance studio, which seemed bigger now that it was just her. High looming ceilings, her own reflection beaming back at her from the bank of mirrors on each side: herself, but not herself. Not the girl who had danced in Aleppo, or in the camp in Kilis, or on the beach at Izmir. Not even the same girl she had been when she first arrived in Manchester. A different girl, one she barely knew.

"So, Aya, is it?" asked the man with the small moustache and large bow tie. Miss Eve had said he was the principal ballet master, Mr Bougeard.

"Yes," Aya said, the word sounding thick on her tongue.

"You are from..." He looked down at his piece of paper, then raised an eyebrow as he said, "Aleppo?"

"Yes."

"Ah, yes – I recall... You're the girl who missed the preliminaries, right?"

Aya nodded.

"It says here you trained with Adriana Belova," said the elegant older lady with the purple bob. Madam Olenska, director of the school.

"You know Madam Belova?" Aya looked at her in surprise.

"Ballet knows no borders, my dear," Madam Olenska said with a smile. "I watched Adriana dance in Jerusalem and I have seen the work her company was doing before the war. You were lucky to have such a teacher. What is she doing now, I wonder?"

Aya stared at the woman in surprise. "Madam Belova is... She's – OK?"

"I heard she was in Dubai," said Miss Eve. "Involved in some very interesting new work, devising a ballet with refugees in one of the border camps."

"Part of a new commissioned piece about the war, I believe," Mr Bougeard was saying. "Knowing Adriana, it promises to be very exciting."

Aya wanted to know more, about her beloved Madam – about the ballet she was choreographing. But then they were asking her about England and her mind was racing to catch up, and all the time her thoughts were tugging back to Mumma... The caseworker had explained that if the appeal was rejected they would be taken to the detention centre while arrangements were made for them to be deported. Would that happen today? Tomorrow? Would there be time to say goodbye?

"So now you train with Helena Rosenberg?" Madam Olenksa was saying. "You have indeed been very fortunate. To work with two such celebrated dancers."

"Yes," said Aya. She wished that more words would come out of her. They must think she could barely speak English, and even though it didn't matter any more, she didn't want these people to see her that way.

"And you have suffered a leg injury," Mr Bougeard was saying, looking down at the papers in front of him. "But Miss Helena believes it is fully healed. May we see?"

The sun was just a little lower now, slanting across the floorboards so that dust motes danced in the shafts of light. Aya remembered the dust in the street after the bomb fell. Remembered how they had all been covered in a sheen of white – like ghost children, moving in slow motion through the rubble-strewn streets. Red blood pouring from her leg and mixing with the dust. Little Ifima lying motionless, like a porcelain doll, in the street. She gulped hard, reminding herself to breathe as the memories rose to drown her.

"Step forward, please." Madam Olenska was watching her intently as she stood up and made her way round the desk, moving with the grace and poise of a prima ballerina. "First position."

Aya obeyed the command without thinking, turning out her feet and holding her arms in the oval shape she had been taught when she was just five years old. She couldn't get the picture of Ifima's face out of her mind. Kimi holding her in her arms, rocking her in the dust.

"Nice turn-out," said Madam Olenska. "Point to second, please."

Aya did as she was told and she felt Madam Olenska's eyes running the length of her leg, almost as if she were measuring the angles of her body – taking in the compact muscles at the top of her thighs, the slight bend of the leg, the scarring along her calf. She remembered the screaming pain. The blood running down her leg, empurpling the dust.

"Please take off your shoes."

Aya took off the ballet shoes Miss Helena had given her and presented her feet. Madam Olenska bent down and took each foot into her hands, one at a time, bending them, shaping them almost like clay. Aya noticed that her long, slender fingers were beautiful to look at, even though they were pale and covered in liver spots. They reminded her of Madam Belova's hands, holding on to the barre so tightly when the bombs fell.

"Nice arches … supple. Though I think you can probably get more bend in this right foot … and your toes… Yes, the three big toes almost the same length… Nice."

Miss Eve spoke for the first time. "It helps with pointe work if your three toes are the same length."

Aya remembered Madam Belova saying the same thing when she showed her the first pair of pointe shoes. That felt like a lifetime ago.

"Thank you." Madam Olenska had released her and was on her feet. "Now, can you show us your dance."

The objects were laid out across the studio floor. The piece of rubble, Moosa's sock, the ballet shoe, Dad's handkerchief. They lay like pieces of driftwood on the vast wooden ocean of floorboards, and as the music started Aya felt like she had when she'd stared out at Dotty's pool.

The opening bars of the music started and Aya remained motionless. Her heart was beating so fast she could feel it in her head.

How could she dance when so many of her friends would never get the chance to dance again? When it meant remembering home – and all she had lost. When it meant reaching out to Dad across the wooden waves, when the memories lapped so close she wasn't sure she could let go of them without being swept up and drowned in them.

More notes playing, dancing over her static form, but still Aya was frozen, unable to move.

How could she dance when Mumma and Moosa were going to be deported? Sent back – where to? To Syria? Aleppo? To a home that no longer existed. To the camp at Kilis? This was probably her last day here. Her last day in Manchester, last day with Dotty, last chance to dance … yet she could not make her body move.

Then suddenly the music had stopped and Madam Olenska was waving her hand in the air.

"Do you need a moment?" It was the man who was speaking. The man with the moustache and the funny bow tie. Aya suddenly couldn't remember his name.

She nodded. No words coming out. Memories buzzed all around her and Aya had the same dizzy feeling she'd had when she'd been locked in the studio, and when she'd been at the pool, as if she couldn't seem to breathe, the roaring sound of panic in her ears. Only worse than either of those times. Worse because it wouldn't stop. Wouldn't go away. And then there was more talk and then a feeling like a curtain coming down in her head, and the next thing she knew she could hear voices – she had no idea whose – saying, "She's passed out!"

Chapter 40

When she woke up she was lying in a small room that she thought was perhaps the school nurse's office – there were posters round the walls that were not about ballet, but about things like "Healthy Diet" and "Why it's important to drink lots of water". Miss Helena was sitting on the other side of the room. When Aya stirred she smiled. "Ah, you are with us again!"

"What … what happened?"

"You fainted. Clean away! Like a candle blown out – poof!"

"Oh no." Aya sat up quickly and immediately felt dizzy again. "I've let you down. I have let everyone down."

Miss Helena placed a hand on her arm. "No, no.

These things – they happen. The heat, the excitement. Here."

She handed Aya some tea in a thin plastic cup and helped her up. She sat with her legs dangling off the bed and stared down at the hot brown liquid. The dizzy feeling was receding a little but she felt exhausted and tearful.

"If you wish, when you feel better, you may try again," said Miss Helena.

"I do, I..." Now that the opportunity had been snatched away from her, Aya suddenly realised how desperately she wanted it. How much she wanted to dance. How much she suddenly, desperately wanted to get into the school.

"But for now you are to drink your tea and eat a biscuit – here." She handed Aya a small plate containing a couple of chocolate biscuits. "And I am going to tell you the end of my story. And you are going to listen. And then – only then – you may decide what you want to do."

Miss Helena sat down. She had the same expression in her eyes as the night when she had told Aya of her journey on the Kindertransport.

Aya took a sip of the tea, which tasted warm and sweet. The room still felt as if it was swimming as her dance teacher started to talk.

"I told you that I came to England on the children's transport in 1939," said Miss Helena. "What I didn't tell you was that my sister Elsa was supposed to come too."

Aya had a strange feeling listening to her. As if time had stood still and the audition, the appeal, were on pause, suspended, waiting for this story to be told.

"There was a confusion at the station. There was only room for one of us. Elsa insisted that I go on without her." Miss Helena paused, smiling a little as she recalled. "I remember that I cried. I was very angry. I didn't want to get on that train on my own and I didn't see why my sister was to stay with my parents when I was not."

Miss Helena smiled again but it was a sad smile, Aya thought. "I see now that she was being very kind, but that is not what I was thinking at the time, I can tell you!"

Aya took another sip of the tea and nibbled on one of the biscuits, sending a little jolt of sugar through her body.

"Elsa promised me that she would come on the very next train. That she could come and find me as soon as she got to England." Miss Helena stood up and moved towards the window where she stood gazing out towards the green sweep of the fields beyond. "The Robertsons had, in fact, agreed to take us both, you see. There was just an error on the paperwork."

Aya thought of all the bits of paper she had encountered on the way to England – forms, and applications, and more forms. Just lines and patterns in pen and ink – but they could shape your destiny. They could be the difference between home and homelessness, safety and danger, life and death.

"What happened?" she managed to ask. "To Elsa?"

"She did get on the next train." Miss Helena continued to look out of the window. "Though I didn't find that out till many years later. It left Prague on the first of September, 1939, you see. It was the last transport to leave the city. There were a hundred and one children on it. But it was turned away when it reached the border. Sent back."

"Why?" Aya's heart was beating fast, her head clearing with the sweet tea and the chocolate and the fresh air from the open window.

"Because war broke out that very day. The borders were closed and there was no escape."

Aya thought of the girl in the picture, the girl with the pigtails, trapped in a city at war. She wondered if any of her own friends were still in Syria, still in Aleppo, where fighting raged on ruthlessly and relentlessly.

"So Elsa stayed in Prague? Until the end of the war?"

Miss Helena smiled as she turned back to Aya, but her face looked tired and sad. "No, she was sent to the Theresienstadt ghetto, along with my parents. This is where the Nazis sent all the Jews. It was not a nice place. Very little food, much disease. Many died there. And those who did not, they were sent to the camps."

"The camps?"

"So many died in the war." Miss Helena's face was creased with sadness now. "Millions of Jews needlessly sent to their deaths. My mother died in the ghetto; my sister and my father were sent to the gas chambers in Auschwitz."

Aya was silent. The humming of the lawnmower outside, the buzzing of a bluebottle against the windowpane, the hammering of her own heart. "How did you … find out?"

"When the war was over, I waited to hear from them. Weeks, months, I waited. Then Mr Robertson said there was a way to trace missing relatives. I think he probably knew by then, but I still hoped."

Miss Helena shook her head and Aya looked at her. So much of what she was going through, the older lady had experienced too.

"After we found out ... what had happened ... I did not want to dance any more," said Miss Helena. "I felt so much guilt. Why had I been given a chance of life when my parents, my own sister had not? For a long time, I would not dance."

Aya looked at her. "That is what I feel. How can I dance if my family are sent away? When so many of my friends have not made it?"

"This is hard," said Miss Helena. "Very hard. You have been given a chance for happiness when others have been robbed of theirs. When others continue to suffer. This is very hard."

"If Mumma and Moosa are deported, how can I stay?"

Miss Helena came to sit down next to Aya on the bed, her voice different now – more certain. "For a long time I did not dance. But then one day I realised something. I heard a piece of music. It was a piece Elsa loved to dance to. My sister Elsa was a far better dancer than me. But she had been robbed of her chance. And that was when I realised that I had to make the most of mine."

Aya looked up at her dance teacher, but what she saw was a young girl, like herself, coming to England – only without any family. How lonely that must have been.

"I worked harder than I ever would have done for myself, because I worked for her. Always, I danced for Elsa – and sometimes that hurt a great deal. It broke my heart to think of her."

"How did you survive when your heart was breaking like that?"

"I danced through it," said Miss Helena. "I danced with it. And if I could turn that heartbreak into dance, it felt as if I could honour it – honour her – and make something beautiful out of the ugliness that had destroyed my Elsa."

"I see," said Aya. The cup of tea was still in her hand and she stared down at it, trying to make sense of all Miss Helena had told her. "But I promised my father I would look after them ... if anything happened. I promised."

"I did not know your father," said Miss Helena. "And I will not presume to speak for him, or to tell you what to do. But I do believe that there is a way to look forward while also honouring the sacrifices others have made for us."

Aya continued to watch the steam rise off the brown liquid.

"There is – I believe – a way to live without breaking

faith with those who have gone. Or those who continue to suffer. And there are more ways to keep a promise than might at first appear."

Aya looked up again at the old woman who was also, somehow, the young Helena – the frightened little girl who had arrived in England all alone and who had made something beautiful out of the life that had been saved for her, as well as the tragedy that surrounded her.

"Can I try again?" she asked. "Will they let me?"

"Of course," said Miss Helena. "Now, drink your tea – and eat that biscuit before I eat it for you!"

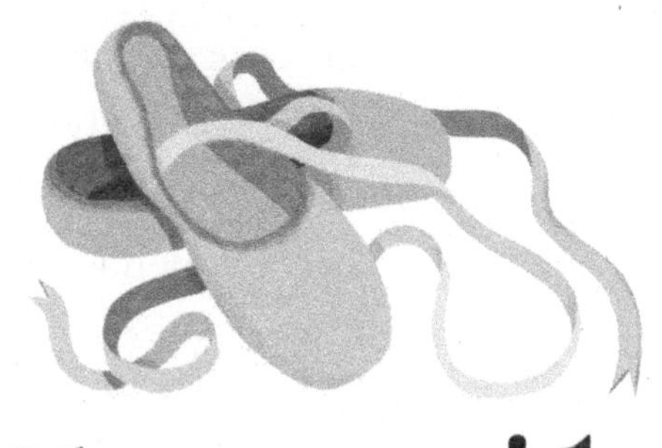

Chapter 41

For the second time that day, Aya lay on the floor in her opening position. The teachers had quietly allowed her to lay out her objects again, and this time she did it slowly, carefully, looking at each one as she laid it down. And now as the music began to play she allowed it to lift her. It was going to hurt – she knew that now – but she also knew she could survive it. Because she wasn't doing it for herself now.

She danced for Moosa first of all – recalling his first faltering steps, his cries in the night, the way he held her fingers so tight and muttered her name in his sleep, the way he needed her, and how much that frightened her, how she resented it sometimes.

Then she turned to the piece of rock that was all she

had left of home, and she danced for all her friends from Aleppo – for Samia, Kimi and Ifima, for Nadiya and Nooda, who might never get this chance that she had. For the boys on the street they had played football with, for the teachers at school – even the horrid maths teacher with the big belly. And she danced for the city itself – the sights and the sounds and the smells that she had loved so much. Yes, the bombs had rained down and there had been so much fear and death, but there had been laughter too and community and a childhood full of memories that all the shelling could never destroy.

The ballet shoe was easy. It made her think of Madam Belova, but also of the dance studio in Manchester – the feeling it gave her of coming home, of new friends and the blessed beautiful release of music. She danced for Miss Helena and Miss Sylvie who had let her in and helped her come back to life – for her new friends who had treated her like one of them – for Dotty and Blue and Lilli-Ella, Grace – even for Ciara.

She danced for Mumma – for the woman who had laughed in the kitchen and said, "Dance for us, *habibti.*" For the happiness she had lost along the way and the colour that was slowly returning to her cheeks. For the bravery she had shown and the pain she had been unable to conceal. For the people at the centre who had lifted her up – Mr Abdul, the Massouds, the food-bank ladies, Sally … the kindness of strangers.

The handkerchief and the shell were last. She felt a chill ripple through her as she turned to them. This part of the dance was for Dad. But the final bit of the memory had been locked away so tight she felt as if she had lost the key to it. But as she took the first step the key slipped into the lock and the memories fell out upon the waves of music. And it wasn't as bad as she had feared.

"Dad! Dad!"

She screamed out to him across the waves. The boat was upturned and he was nowhere to be seen on the black heaving ocean.

"Aya! My Aya!"

And then there he was, calling her name too, then reaching her and pulling her towards the upturned hull of the boat, telling her to hold on to the rope and not let go. Mumma too. And Moosa. He was there. He was OK!

Somehow they survived a whole night on the water after the boat had capsized. She barely had any recollection of those long hours. She remembered only the coldness and the huge vast blackness of ocean and sky. She had felt sometimes as if she had disappeared, obliterated by the night, lost in it. And yet the thing that had kept her awake, kept her holding on to the capsized shell of the boat had been Dad. He had been there all night, holding her, talking to her, telling them all to hang on, that it would be OK. She remembered him telling her the story of the dancing princess who had never stopped dancing all night and all day, through fiery monsters and dragons and battlefields. Dancing over hot coals and ice and stormy seas … dancing, always dancing. And Dad's soft voice saying over and over, "Don't give up, don't let go – keep holding on to the rope, holding on to your dreams, habibti*! Never let go."*

She recalled the dawn rising over the water. When she could no longer feel her own body but she could feel Dad's arms still round her as they caught sight of the little fishing vessel sliding across the waves. Aya was too cold, half frozen, unable to take in what was happening.

There was not enough space for everyone. Women and children only. Then Dad was letting go and she felt strong arms round her, pulling her out of the water, away from Dad.

She had called his name. Desperate. "Dad! No!"

"Go to England," he said. "Take Moosa and Mumma. I will follow. I promise!"

At least, that's what she thought he had said. The memory was blurry, watermarked. But as she danced that day in the big old studio, she saw Dad's face again – clearly, not in fragments – and he was telling her to go – telling her he would follow, telling her to live, telling her never to let go of her dreams. And on the ocean that was the wooden studio floor, Aya reached out to him again, and just for a fleeting moment it was as if Dad was there with her in the studio, holding her hand, his almond eyes fixed on hers, saying, "Dance, *habibti*! Dance. And never stop dancing."

And so she pulled away, turned from him with one last anguished glance, willed her body into a pirouette and turned, turned, turned towards the future.

Chapter 42

She and Dotty were both silent for most of the car journey home. Aya stared out of the window as they passed green hedgerows and fields, bright with golden harvest, rippling towards unbroken blue English skies. Dotty wound down the window and stuck her head out, and Aya could smell the rich rasp of the earth, the green sap of the trees. It was so different from the smell of Aleppo in the summer but today, for some reason, it smelled like home. The thought of leaving it tore at her like claws in her belly but she drank it in – allowed herself to feel it, the joy and the pain both.

Aya hadn't told Dotty of the phone conversation that she had overheard. She wanted to enjoy this last time with her friend. There was no sign of Mumma when they got back to the house, so the girls went out to the garden and sat under the giant beech tree, staring up at the canopy of leaves dancing, in patterns that were almost like water.

"My dance went OK, I think," said Dotty. "I actually kind of enjoyed it – I think cos it's not exactly ballet. I mean, it was, but I felt as if I was able to have fun with it, so I forgot to be stressed, which probably means my technique was all over the place, but at least I didn't burst into tears like I thought I would."

"I cannot imagine you crying," said Aya, glancing at Dotty, who was picking daisies off the lawn and stripping them of their petals.

"They love us – they love us not," said Dotty, plucking off the white petals one at a time and tossing them aside. Dotty glanced at her then and Aya held her eye. "What will you do if…"

Dotty didn't finish the sentence. She didn't need to. Both of them knew what she meant.

Aya didn't get a chance to answer, because then came the sound of a car drawing up, and voices on the drive, and then there was Mumma, crossing the lawn with Moosa in her arms and a smile on her face. She was talking fast in Arabic, so fast Aya could not take in what she was saying. It didn't make sense.

"We can really stay?" Aya repeated, barely able to take in the momentous news. "But I thought… Miss Helena was saying…"

"There was some confusion at first," Mr Buchanan explained. "It seemed your case was going to be turned down on the grounds that you had already applied for asylum in Greece."

Aya recalled Miss Helena's words. *"At least this way she has a chance to audition before they are deported."*

"But I had asked a friend at the Home Office to help," Mr Buchanan said. "He got to the bottom of things – said it was a fairly simple case in the end. Frustrating, really. I suspect there are hundreds of families in the same situation. Legally entitled to remain but unable to navigate the complex immigration system. It makes me angry."

"So we can stay? We can really stay?"

"Yes, we can stay," said Mumma, and she said it in English, the four words thick and unfamiliar on her tongue.

Aya laughed. "When are you learning English, Mumma?"

"Bronte – she teach," said Mumma, in English again, tripping over the thick clotted sounds and breaking into a smile as she looked at Dotty's mother, who was more elegant than usual today, in a navy shift dress with a string of what looked like real pearls.

"Mum, you are a teacher now!" laughed Dotty.

"No need to sound so surprised , darling!"

Dotty was dancing around excitedly. "So will you stay here? Forever?"

"I hope so," said Miss Helena. "This house is far too big for two old ladies. We are rattling around in it!"

"She's right," said Miss Sylvie. "This is a garden that needs children to climb trees and a house with corners for hide-and-seek."

Aya translated all this for her mother with tears in her eyes. "You are sure?" she said. "It seems ... too much..."

Miss Helena put a hand out and touched her flushed cheek. It had been such a confusing and complicated day. "My dear, this house became my home when my own was lost to me," she said. "Let it be the same for you now. A way of honouring the tradition. After all, there should have been two girls here – two young dancers, but only one made it."

Aya understood and smiled. Perhaps if history was always repeating itself – wars and families fleeing their homes, persecution, refugees – then other stories recurred too: stories of kindness, sacrifice, generosity.

What had Miss Helena called it? The kindness of strangers. Decade after decade. Generation after generation. Making the world a better place.

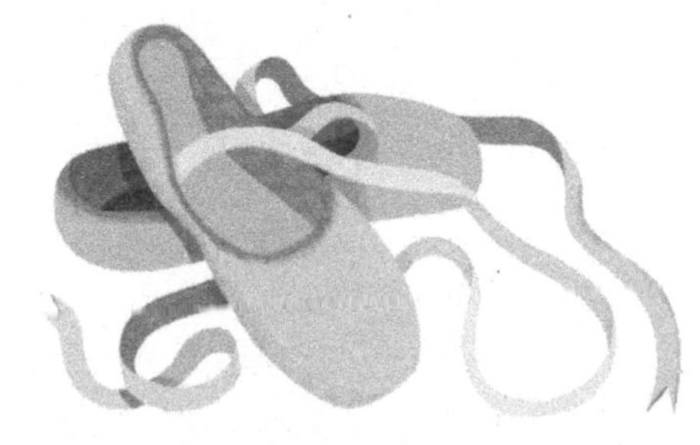

Chapter 43

They had been told it would be at least a week before there was any news about the audition but luckily the next few days were filled with preparations for the concert. Everyone was involved in helping – baking cakes, organising a raffle, collecting donations for the food bank, making costumes, rehearsing, getting the stage ready.

In any case, Aya was in no hurry to hear. "I wasn't even trying in the audition class," she said, as she and Dotty were painting signs to go up outside the hall on the day of the concert. "And I can't really remember what I did in my dance."

"I can," said Dotty. "And the memories aren't all good, I can tell you! Madam Olenska said my dance was ‘unconventional’ and the Bougeard man actually laughed out loud at one point. That can’t be a great sign!”

“There’s always next year!” said Aya. Next year, or the year after, or the year after. Now there was no longer the threat of deportation, she could let her dreams spread out into a long distant future. And yet … Oh, if only she could go there now!

“Not for me,” said Dotty, who had managed to get paint in her hair and all over her clothes. “I told Mum last night that if I don’t get in then I don’t want to be a dancer.”

“Really? What did she say?”

“Nothing! She burst into tears and she hasn’t spoken to me since,” said Dotty, adopting a tragic expression that Aya suspected was closer to the truth than she intended. “My dad was passing messages between us at breakfast. It’s basically like a war zone in my house… Oh!” Her expression changed suddenly. “I am so sorry. I didn’t mean…”

Aya glanced at her friend. Dotty had not experienced war, or bombing. She had not lived in a war zone. But she was frightened of losing her mother too. And Aya knew how that felt.

“Maybe it will all work out,” said Aya.

"Maybe," said Dotty. "But I don't even know if I want to get in or not! Mum will probably disown me if I don't but if I do … then I have to go!"

The two girls looked at each other and both sighed at the same time. "Well, we will find out soon enough," said Aya.

"And till then, we have a show to get on the road!" said Dotty, adopting a ringmaster pose and raising an imaginary top hat. "So let's get this party started, baby!"

The show was, in fact, coming together very well. Mr Abdul had designed posters that the girls had stuck up in local shops and businesses, many of whom also donated raffle prizes. Bronte Buchanan may not have been speaking to her daughter, but she had agreed to do a star turn, which meant that the local newspapers and radio stations were all running stories on the event. One magazine even wanted to do a story on Aya herself, the refugee ballerina who was the inspiration behind the concert.

"It might help with trying to trace your dad," Mr Buchanan had explained when Aya looked nervous. "All publicity is good publicity!"

"Is there any news?" Aya asked. She had a spot of

purple paint on her cheek from painting the posters earlier and Mr Buchanan thought that she seemed to have so much more colour than the pallid little girl who had stood terrified by the pool, though she still had the wary look in her eyes that he wondered if she would ever really lose.

"We are doing all we can," he said.

His friend in the Home Office had managed to trace Mr and Mrs Massoud's son, Jimi, who was being held in jail in Damascus as a political prisoner. Mrs Massoud had cried when they told her. "I always knew he was alive and yet I also did not believe it till this moment," she said.

"There is no prospect of his release any time soon," Mr Buchanan explained. "Things are very complicated."

"But he is alive, and while there is life there is hope," said Mrs Massoud. And her husband – who rarely said anything; who let his wife speak for him – buried his head in his hands and burst into tears. *A father's tears flow forever too*, Aya thought to herself.

Souda Refugee Camp, Chios Island, Greece

They were in the camp on Chios for over three months. Waiting.

Waiting. Waiting for Dad. Waiting to be assigned a relocation country. Waiting to be moved on. The waiting ate into your soul after a while, thought Aya. Made you feel as if you were not really alive, barely breathing, invisible.

And there was nowhere to dance there. And no music in Aya's soul even if there had been. She wondered, sitting on the beach every day, watching for Dad, if she would ever want to dance again.

Eventually they were assigned papers by the UNHCR to fly to England. There were medical tests and an orientation session and then they were moved into a hotel room for a night before the flight. The next morning there were more tests and interviews to check they were fit to travel. Then they were accompanied to the airport and put on a special flight with a group of other women and children who looked as disorientated as they were.

Nobody spoke the whole way there.

Moosa cried in Aya's arms as the plane took off and Mumma sat in silence next to them. Aya looked out of the window, at the clouds and the sea below. All she could think of was Dad. What if today was the day he came? What if he came and she wasn't there? Wasn't waiting for him?

What if he never found them? What if she never saw him again?

Chapter 44

Aya was surprised at how nervous she was before the concert. They had spent most of the day decorating the hall, transforming it from a tattered community centre into a venue for a ballet recital: putting out the rows of chairs, setting up tables for the cake stall and the raffle and the tombola. Mr Massoud had mended the curtains so they now opened and closed when you pulled the ropes, and Mrs Massoud had made bunting from old scraps of material found backstage. Lilli-Ella and Grace had baked mountains of flapjacks and brownies; Blue had made large jugs of home-made lemonade; and each of the little girls had donated gifts for the raffle. One of the parents had donated a giant teddy bear – twice the size of Aya

– which was the first prize.

The girls were using the dance studio upstairs as a dressing room and it was absolute chaos, with small dancers dressed up as cats chasing each other's tails while Dotty and Aya and the older ones tried to make them sit down for make-up whiskers.

The older girls were starting with a piece from *The Nutcracker* that Madam Helena had taught them – a medley of dances from the full-length ballet. But there was no sign of Ciara, who had agreed – reluctantly – to dance the Sugar Plum Fairy.

"Do you think she's just ditched the whole thing?" asked Dotty.

"She did keep saying what a waste of time it all is," said Lilli-Ella.

"She says stuff like that when she's nervous," observed Grace.

"Nervous?" said Dotty.

"She was worried – at the audition." Aya said. Ciara hadn't said anything about how her audition had gone in the days since it had happened. In fact, she had barely talked to Aya at all.

"She hasn't got anything to worry about," said Dotty, pulling a face. "She's totally in there. She knows it. We all know it."

Aya shrugged, remembering how terrified Ciara had seemed in the class, and what her mother had said when they arrived at the audition.

The door opened then and Ciara came in, her face pale and her eyes red, as if she'd been crying.

"Are you OK?" asked Blue.

"Fine." Ciara sniffed. "I just need to get on with this show, then I can go home."

"You don't look great," said Lilli-Ella, looking concerned.

"I just have hay fever, OK?" Ciara snapped.

Aya looked at her. Ciara's face was blotchy and her eyes were flat and blank. She wanted to say something but Ciara just turned away.

The community centre was filling up and when Dotty peeked down the stairs she reported that nearly all the seats were full. "Dad says it will be standing room only soon! Come on, you lot. We need to be ready to give our public a performance to remember!"

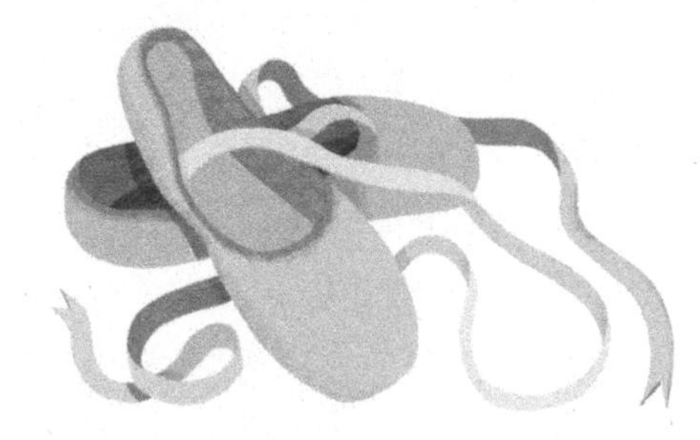

Chapter 45

Miss Helena opened the show by introducing Sally from Manchester Welcomes Refugees, who spoke briefly about the work of the charity and how people in the community could help. Then the girls performed their *Nutcracker* piece. It was funny to step out on to the stage and see the audience assembled on chairs. So many unfamiliar faces, but a few familiar ones too: the food-bank ladies, Mr and Mrs Massoud, and Mr Abdul, who was sitting next to Miss Helena, looking very pleased with himself. Even the tired-looking caseworker had a smile on his face today.

When the music started, Aya forgot about them all and just enjoyed herself. She played just a small role in this piece, with Ciara taking the lead, but it felt so good to dance again, with her new friends around her, in a place she was starting to be able to call home.

They received stampedes of applause at the end, and they all came off stage on a high, giggling and laughing as they pulled off one set of costumes and changed into another. One of the younger classes was on now, performing a tap dance routine, with Blue, Lilli-Ella – and Mr Abdul. They were all wearing top hats, which kept falling off in rehearsal but which somehow, miraculously, seemed to stay put in the real show.

Then the little girls were up with the cat dance that Dotty and Aya had taught them. Margot lost her tail and little Ainka entirely forgot the moves and just stood there smiling and wiggling, but the audience loved it.

Then the little cats all remained on stage to accompany Dotty in her musical theatre medley. She had been working on it on her own and hadn't shown it to anyone, so this was the first time that Aya had ever seen her friend perform quite like this. First she was Sillabub the young kitten, singing of her hopes and dreams, then she transformed into Gus, the old Theatre Cat, paws shaking with palsy and old age, then Macavity – the Mystery Cat – the master criminal and daredevil, delighting the audience with his exploits. With each transformation she danced a different style, the steps reflecting the character of each cat so perfectly it made Aya gasp.

Then the music changed and Dotty shape-shifted one more time – now she was Grizabella, the shabby old grey cat, lonely and tormented by memories, singing to the moon. You could have heard a pin drop in the community centre as Dotty sang, the plaintive notes soaring, full of loss and longing. When she finished there was absolute silence for what felt like forever, and then the audience were on their feet, stamping and cheering. Aya realised that she had tears running down her face, and when she looked at her friend, she saw Dotty did too.

She looked out at the audience to see if she could catch a glimpse of Bronte Buchanan, but she was nowhere to be seen.

By the time they reached the interval, all the dancers were high as kites. They peeked out at the audience, who were buying teas and coffees and cakes and raffle tickets, talking animatedly.

"They are all loving the show," said Mrs Massoud, who had come backstage to join them before getting ready for her own performance. "And who can blame them – it is wonderful, wonderful!"

Miss Helena and Miss Sylvie appeared then and

were smiling too. They beckoned Aya, Dotty and Ciara into the office and shut the door. "Girls, I have some news for you," said Miss Helena. "Are you wanting me to tell you now or after the show?"

"It depends what the news is," said Dotty, looking at the envelope in Miss Helena's hand and grimacing.

Miss Helena surveyed her with serious eyes. "Dotty, the school have accepted you, but—" she paused and the "but" seemed to hang in the air for what felt like an eternity "—they want you to join their musical theatre programme."

Dotty let out a gasp. "I – I didn't know they even did one!"

"It's a new initiative, starting next year," Miss Sylvie explained. "For dancers who they think are better suited to the West End than the barre. And after what I just saw on stage, I think they are quite right!"

"That's... OMG, that's awesome!" Dotty looked elated for a second before her face fell. "Only, my mum..."

"Your mum is thrilled for you, darling!" said a voice from the doorway. Dotty turned. Her mother was dressed in a tutu, her hair pulled sharply back from her face and framed with a tiny tiara of feathers. She looked exquisite – and she had tears in her eyes.

"You aren't ... disappointed?" Dotty looked at her anxiously – the way she looked at the invisible figure in her dance, Aya thought. Pleading, hopeful...

"Disappointed? No, I couldn't be prouder – or happier," laughed Bronte Buchanan. "In fact, I rather think they know my daughter better than I do."

"Really?"

"Watching you on stage just now – darling, you told a story and you made the audience's hearts soar and break with yours. That was true artistry!" Bronte Buchanan gazed at her daughter with fierce pride in her eyes. "I am only sorry, darling, that I spent so long making you follow my dream rather than letting you chase your own."

Dotty ran into her mother's arms and Aya watched them holding each other tight, and felt a glow of happiness so bright she felt as if she might burst too.

But then Miss Helena was turning to her and Ciara, and her stomach contracted hard. So many good things had already happened to her. She barely dared hope this dream might come true too.

"Girls," she said, a broad smile in her twinkling old face. "Congratulations, my dancers! You have both been offered a place on the ballet programme."

The words didn't seem to register properly at first.

Could Miss Helena really have just said that she was in? That she was going to the Royal Northern – with Dotty too?

"And, Aya, you have been awarded a full scholarship for board and training," Miss Sylvie added.

Aya's heart soared! She couldn't wait to run downstairs and tell Mumma. But for some reason – just in that first moment – it was her father's face that she could see in her mind's eye. Dad telling her to follow her dreams and never let go.

"I am absolutely delighted for all three of you," said Bronte Buchanan. "And I can't think of anyone who deserves that scholarship more!"

Yarl's Wood Immigration Centre, Bedford

After they arrived in England they had been taken to the detention centre in Bedford. A journey in a police van along grey motorways, through concreted underpasses, past tower blocks and rows of houses.

At the detention centre they had been given a family room with proper beds, and assigned a caseworker who would help them with their asylum application, and help them access medical care and legal support. But there were problems with the papers. And everyone talked so fast in English that Aya had not been able to keep up, and Mumma kept crying. Moosa was always crying too, clinging to Aya all the time, screaming if she let him go.

And they wouldn't let Aya go with Mumma when they interviewed her. Even though Aya said Mumma spoke no English. Everyone was kind enough but they didn't seem to understand. Or they didn't really listen. Not to her – because she was a child. And there were so many other people in the centre – all with the same stories, all looking for refuge. All wanting to be heard.

All looking for a home.

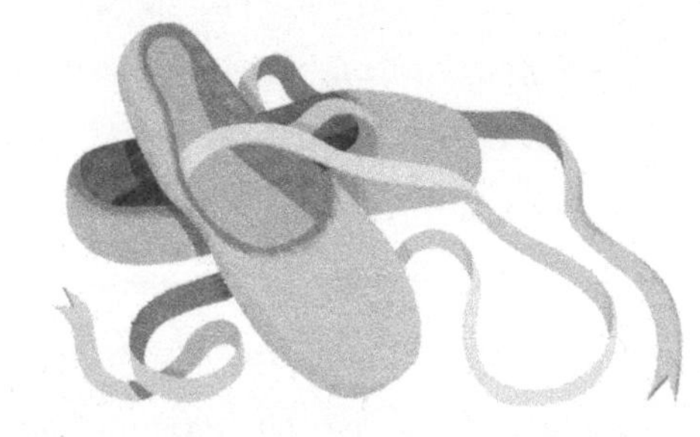

Chapter 46

There was one more thing to do. Before the dancing began again after the interval, Aya had agreed to tell her story. Miss Helena had suggested it and Sally had helped her to write it. Mr Massoud had made a slide show of pictures to represent some of the places she had been on her journey.

Standing up on stage as herself was much harder than doing it as a snowflake or a sugar plum fairy. She could feel the whole hall staring up at her – so many neighbourhood people who didn't know her from a stranger. Who saw her as the other girls had once. As a refugee. An asylum seeker. A migrant. Not a little girl. Or a dancer. Not one of them.

But once she started talking it was easier than she

had thought. Perhaps because she had told the story before – in dance – so remembering things now was easier. Perhaps because they were here in England, and they could stay. And because Mumma had agreed to go and see a counsellor to help her feel less anxious all the time … and Moosa was going to start at nursery … and because Aya had been offered a place at the Royal Northern… Because they had a future now, and that made it easier to talk about the past.

When she got to the bit about Dad – in the ocean – she stopped and her voice cracked. She wasn't sure she would be able to go on. But then Dotty appeared by her side and took her hand. Aya turned to her friend and smiled. Then she took a deep breath and went on.

"We still don't know what happened to him," she said. "Dotty's father – Mr Buchanan – he is helping us, to see if we can trace him. There are organisations that help reunify families and they think that it is possible. That if he is alive we might one day be able to find him. But we don't know."

After she told her story she came off stage. And to her surprise it was Ciara who was the first to give her a hug.

"I'm sorry," she said. "I didn't realise..."

"It is OK," said Aya. "You have your things too."

Ciara shrugged and her eyes filled with tears. "My parents are splitting up. My dad is moving away with his new girlfriend. I know it's not the same as your dad but…"

"But you miss him?"

Ciara nodded.

"I … understand this," said Aya. Neither of them said anything for a moment, but the two girls looked at each other with a new understanding.

"Maybe … I mean, if we are going to school together…" Ciara hesitated. "Can we be … friends?"

Aya smiled. "I would like that," she said. "Very much."

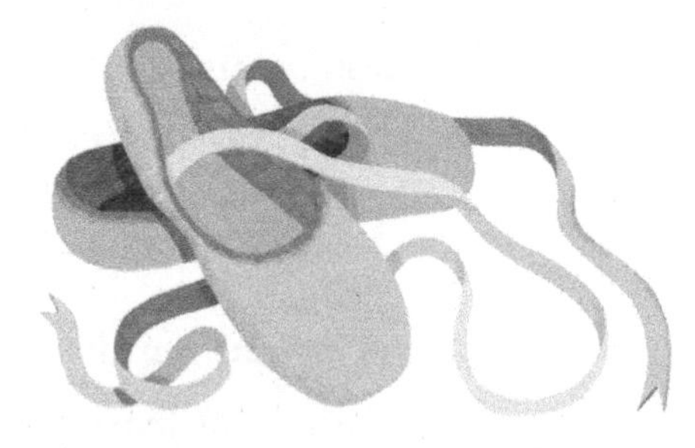

Chapter 47

Bronte Buchanan was going to dance the last piece of the night, but Aya was given the slot before hers. The girls had done their pop song medley dance, and Mr and Mrs Massoud had performed a beautiful waltz. Then Dotty and Ciara had performed their audition solos and now it was Aya's turn. She felt oddly calm as she went on the stage with each of her objects – so different to how she had felt in the audition. And this time when she danced the piece, she danced it as a celebration of the past – not mourning for it, but bringing alive the things that had brought her to where she was today.

From Aleppo ... the container ... the camp in Kilis ... the beach in Izmir ... the journey across the

Med … the tents on Chios … the detention centre in Bedford … then arriving in Manchester, where she first heard the sound of piano notes filtering down from the window upstairs…

She could feel the tears streaming down her face as she danced, but it didn't hurt – at least, not too much. And as she looked out across the room, over the sea of faces, she thought she saw the door to the community centre open, thought she saw the figure of a man in a blue raincoat slip in at the back, a man with a rough beard, a small scar on his chin and her father's almond-shaped eyes.

She knew he wasn't really there; it wasn't really Dad. She knew he might never return, never walk through the door and back into her life, but she allowed herself to see him then, allowed herself to dance for him – for Dad – for one last time.

"We made it, Dad," she told him with her eyes and her fingertips. "We made it and we are safe," she said with the graceful curve of her arms. "We will never stop waiting for you – looking for you. Even if you never come we'll never let go of you – of our memories, of our past," her dance seemed to say. And she could see him smiling back, almond eyes bright with tears. And she was on her toes now, leg extended high behind her in an arabesque, her whole body curved in a perfect line flowing from fingertip to fingertip – past to future.

"So I'm going to follow my dreams, Dad. Make something beautiful out of all this ugliness," the sweep of the dance seemed to tell him. "Because – we made it, Dad. We found – home."

Aya's journey from Syria
IRELAND
6
UNITED KINGDOM
POLAND
GERMANY
FRANCE
AUSTRIA
ITALY
SPAIN
1. ALEPPO, SYRIA
2. KILIS, TURKEY
3. IZMIR, TURKEY
4. MEDITERRANEAN SEA
5. CHIOS, GREECE
6. BEDFORD, ENGLAND

RUSSIA
BELARUS
UKRAINE
ROMANIA
BULGARIA
GREECE
TURKEY
SYRIA
IRAQ
SAUDI ARABIA
1
2
3
4
5

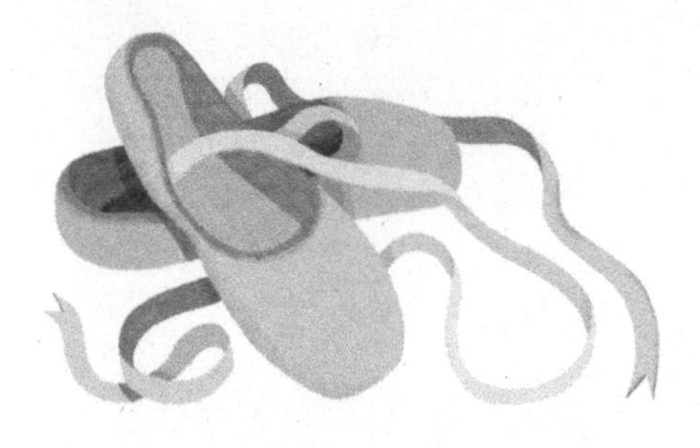

Afterword

When I was eleven I adored Noel Streatfeild's *Ballet Shoes* and Pamela Brown's *The Swish of the Curtain*, and was so fixated on Lorna Hill's *Sadler's Wells* ballet books – each of which I had read at least ten times – that eventually my mum decided enough was enough. She prised my tattered copy of *Veronica at the Wells* out of my hands and gave me a pile of new reading material, which included *The Silver Sword*, *When Hitler Stole Pink Rabbit*, and *The Diary of Anne Frank*. That was when I discovered that there was a new kind of book to love – stories that could open your eyes, change the way you saw the world, make you ask questions, expand your horizons, enrich your soul – switch on lightbulbs in your head!

As an English teacher for the past twenty-five years I have had the great privilege of introducing kids to those 'lightbulb books' – the stories that expand their capacity for empathy and challenge their preconceptions about the world; that help them look at and come to terms with the most difficult issues of growing up in the world today.

And so as an author those are the books I have tried to write.

As the world watched the migrant crisis beginning to unfold I knew it was something I wanted – needed – to write about. Hearing Judith Kerr, the author of *When Hitler Stole Pink Rabbit*, speak about the parallels between her story and the current situation in Syria, I had my own lightbulb moment. I would write about a child displaced from their home by war in Syria, fleeing across Europe, and seeking asylum in the UK. A story that was a modern version of *When Hitler Stole Pink Rabbit* and *The Silver Sword* – a story that would make young readers look beyond the labels of 'refugee' and 'asylum seeker' to see the child behind.

When I discussed the idea with my editor at Nosy Crow, we were both conscious of the difficulties of writing about events that are happening now – complex, potentially troubling issues that we would be asking young readers to confront without the distance of history. I have a quote from one of my favourite writers, Alan Gibbons, above my desk: "I never enter a dark room unless I can light the way out." That's what I wanted to do – to confront difficult issues, in a way that didn't offer glib solutions or whitewash the truth, but which did offer the consolation of hope.

A charity local to me, Bristol Refugee Rights, holds a drop-in at a community centre where dance lessons are also held. I found myself imagining a young Syrian girl, just arrived in the UK, disorientated, not knowing if she'd be allowed to stay, watching a ballet class through a half-open doorway, seeing girls just like her friends from home, longing to be back at her own dance school. The story began from there.

I contacted Bath Welcomes Refugees and other refugee resettlement projects who helped me with research, and I spoke to members of the Syrian community who had come to Britain, as well as reading many, many accounts and transcripts from child refugees, but I did find myself struggling for a long time with the voice. Aya's voice eluded me – sometimes she was there, sometimes she slipped away from me, and tying together her past narrative with her present was particularly challenging. Until I realised that of course it would be – dealing with the past and reconciling it with the present is hugely difficult for many of these children. I made the decision to tell the story of Aya's life in Aleppo – her experiences before and during the war, her flight through Turkey, in a container, in refugee camps, crossing the Med in a storm – all in flashbacks interspersed between the story of her experiences as a young asylum seeker in the UK. At first the two stories are distinct, but gradually dance becomes a medium for Aya to work through complex suppressed memories and the two begin to come together. As she becomes more able to talk about the past and grieve for what's lost – coming to terms with what may have happened to her father – she is also able to begin to let go of the guilt and look to the future.

Telling Aya's story felt like a big responsibility. Sometimes I wondered if it was my story to tell – and I hope that in future years we will see stories of child migrants told by those who lived through it. But it didn't feel like this story could wait. It has to be told now – to this generation who are growing up now. Because when you turn on your TV and see a story about a Syrian refugee who has escaped the horrors of war, only to be attacked in a school in the UK, you realise why it is so important for this generation of young readers to question the toxic definitions attached to words like 'refugee' and 'asylum seeker' – to see the child, not the label.

But I hope this story might also be to young readers what *Ballet Shoes* and *The Swish of the Curtain* and the *Sadler's Wells* series were to me – the stories of following your dreams that I adored and read over and over; that I read to my children and still pick up as old favourites today. My mum doesn't take them off me now! She knows that the moment she pressed those lightbulb books into my hand, she helped me grow up as a reader – but it was the love of both kinds of books that made me a reader for life. If *No Ballet Shoes in Syria* can do that for any young readers, or if a child like Aya can read it and see themselves represented on the pages of a book – their story told, in which they are the heroine, not just a victim – then I will have done what I set out to do.

Acknowledgements

With huge thanks to Annette Hind, Lucy Hind and Karen Paisey of Dorothy Colborne School of Dance, to Sally Harris of Bath Welcomes Refugees, and to Faisal Aljawabra and family, all of whom generously helped me with research. To my favourite young editors, Evie Giachritsis, Elsie Bruton and Lucy Smith. To Jo Nadin, for writing wisdom and general wonderfulness. To my ballet teacher, Patricia Parkinson, for giving me a love of dance; and to Miss Eve and all the dancing girls of Sunshine Ballet School days, with love and fond memories. Thank you to all my colleagues and pupils at King Edward's School, Bath, for endlessly inspiring me, and especially to the head, Martin Boden, for supporting this book and the cause. Thank you to the wonderful Caroline Montgomery of Rupert Crew, who is not only the best agent in the world but a dear friend; to Clare Hall Craggs for championing this book to the world, and to all the team at Nosy Crow, especially Tom Bonnick, for his wisdom and inspiration, without which I could never have written this story. Most of all to Jonny, Joe and Elsie, my favourite people in the world – with love always!